Dedications

To my siblings: Furkan, Yusuf, and Huda for offering countless childhood memories, which have served as great field experience for my books, and to my youngest sister, Meryem, for being my greatest fan and my biggest inspiration. This book is for you.
~ Nur Kose

To my younger self - You were always so full of story ideas, churning them out into books you created with printing paper and pencil. You printed your name on each cover, with confidence that you, just like all your favorite authors, would one day write a book. For you, I never gave up on that dream. I hope I've made you proud.
~ Nura Fahzy

The Summer When Everything Changed

Written by Nur Kose and Nura Fahzy
Illustrated by Nura Fahzy
Edited by Safa Ahmed

PROLANCE

The Summer When Everything Changed

Prologue

Okay, Ameerah. Listen up. You've got this.

I placed my hand on the giant red door of the gym. Through the narrow window in the door, I gazed at the endless rows of people filling the bleachers. Six girls, dressed in blue and white, stood chatting on one side of the court. *That's us*, I told myself.

One girl was missing from the group of six. One more girl, wearing blue and white, was left to join the group and make it seven. To complete our basketball team. I glanced down at my jersey and sweats. *That's me.*

I tried to slow down the intense pounding of my heart. The game had barely even started, yet I was sweating as if it had. Normally, I wouldn't feel as nervous before a basketball game, but today was different. Today was the last game of the season. I couldn't let anybody down.

I took a deep breath and pushed open the door. Bismillah.[1]

---

[1] In the name of God.

Chapter 1
Hanaan

A warm breeze murmured around me, ruffling strands of my long black hair. I hugged my knees tighter to my chest, murmuring my morning adhkar[2] as I soaked in the lovely morning. My gaze roamed around the familiar sight of my neighborhood, a sight I had grown accustomed to with time. The shadowy trees pushed against the sky, nearly blending into its darkness. A small glow along the horizon promised the arrival of the sun, slowly yet surely. The neat rows of houses lined on the street remained fast asleep.

And then, just as I expected, I heard it. I heard everything. The song of the morning. Birds, joyful and energized, flew out from their nests and branches, feeding their own music to the morning singsong. The tree leaves rustled, whispering among themselves. My sister's voice, carrying the beautiful verses of the Qur'an, drifted outside and into my ears. The words touched my heart, sending a sense of serenity throughout my body. Content, I closed my eyes, reminding myself again why I loved Fajr's Shadow so much.

"Fajr's Shadow" was the name I had given to my special place at age nine, when I was eager to give a name to anything and everything I loved. My room overlooked our front yard, and right below my window ledge stood the roof of our veranda. The roof extended across the length of the house, its wood painted a dark

---

[2]Supplication

shade of blue. It was wide enough for me to crawl out of my window every morning to gaze at the world around me, and to simply think. Having this special place was the only reason I finally moved out of my older sister's room after I turned eight. My parents had been trying to convince me for months by offering to buy me a brand new bed or repaint the office room to colors of my choice. However, I refused to leave the comfort of my sister's room no matter what. That is, until I discovered Fajr's Shadow.

After Fajr[3] is my favorite time to sit alone and think. I love to imagine stories about everything around me and simply listen to the comforting sounds of the early morning. I remain in my special place until the sun rises and the neighborhood begins to wake up. Mr. Roberts leaving for work is my cue to return to my room, refreshed and bursting with inspiration. And then, I write.

I write anything that I can think of: creative dialogues between the birds and the flowers, adventurous stories about exciting characters, imaginary letters between unique people, and reflections about nature that I put in my "Fajr Prose" box. My writings have a cheerful undertone because sitting in Fajr's Shadow always puts me in a pleasant mood, full of energy and unharnessed joy to begin a new day.

At least, that was true until the summer I turned twelve. That was the summer I wrote a poem titled "Betrayal." It was also the summer Ameerah entered my life.

---

[3]Dawn prayer

Chapter 2
Ameerah

Watching my favorite ice cream flavors being scooped into their typical chocolate waffle cone had to be my number one favorite pastime. I hadn't even taken the cone yet, but I could already taste the delicious strawberry cheesecake melting in my mouth, with the addition of the soft orange sorbet that never failed to awaken my palate. I bounced on my toes, impatient for Sister Tesneem, my coach, to pay for the cones.

My best friend, Sherine, was awaiting her cone as well; a single scoop of vanilla topped with chocolate sauce and a cherry. Loose strands of her curly auburn hair hung in front of her face. Beads of sweat lingered on her neck from the basketball game we'd won earlier, which explained the ice cream outing.

This was the third game we'd won in a row, and my whole team had been given trophies. To celebrate our victory, our coach had brought us out for ice cream.

"Sherine, Ameerah!" called Sister Tesneem. "Come and get it!"

Sherine and I hurried over to grab our cones. "Thank you so much, Sister Tesneem!" I smiled at my coach.

"Yes, thank you!" Sherine piped up, heaving a satisfied sigh.

Our coach smiled. "You girls earned it. What can I say?" Slipping her credit card back inside her flip case wallet, she thrust her chin towards the entrance. "Let's head outside, team!"

Sister Tesneem brought us outside of the building and sat us down at one of the vacant tables. I settled down into one of the familiar plastic gray seats which matched the smooth, round table, protected from the sun by a light blue umbrella.

The day was beautiful, to say the least. Everything outside of the shade was touched by the radiant sunshine. A rainbow of cars hurried down the street every now and then, sunlight reflecting on the glitter-like metal.

I nodded after a lick of my ice cream. "Mmm. This ice cream is good."

Sherine laughed. "Are you surprised? You order that combo every time you come here."

I laughed. "Yes, true. I'm not surprised. I'm just stating a fact."

"I still can't process how you would think mixing strawberry cheesecake with orange sorbet tastes good, but you do you, girl."

"You should try it sometime," I replied. "Try something out of your comfort zone, you know."

Sherine tipped her head to the side. "Maaaybe. Maybe someday."

When we'd finally finished our cones, we all thanked our coach again for the ice cream. "You're welcome," she replied. "Now, do any of you girls need a ride home?"

The rest of my teammates shook their heads. I raised my hand. "My brothers are supposed to come and get me," I said. "May I use your phone to call them?"

Sister Tesneem nodded to me. "Yes, Ameerah, you may." She fished her phone out of her pocket and handed it to me. I dialed my eldest brother. The phone rang five times, then went to voicemail.

"Your call has been forwarded to an automated voice-message system. To leave a message——"

I hung up before the operator could say any more. Not surprised since Abdel-Hakeem typically wasn't good about responding to phone calls, I dialed my other brother, and this time the phone rang twice before I heard Ali's voice.

"Assalamu alaikum, Ameerah[4]. Are you finished?"

"Wa alaikumussalam[5]!" I said. "Yes, I'm at Polar Point right now with my team."

"Ice cream?" he asked. "You won again?" I could hear the smile in his voice.

"Yes, we did! Third time in a row!"

My brother laughed. "Congratulations! I'm proud of you. Listen, we're about five minutes away, so insha Allah[6] we'll swing by to get you, alright?"

"Sure," I said. "See you then!"

"Sounds good, princess. Assalamu alaikum."

"Wa alaikumussalam," I giggled.

After Ali hung up, I gave the phone back to Sister Tesneem and said, "My brothers will come in five minutes."

My coach slid the phone back into her pocket. "Alright, cool."

"We should probably take your stuff out of the car, then," said Mina.

---

[4]Peace be upon you

[5]And peace be upon you, too

[6]If God wills

"Mina is right," said Sister Tesneem. "C'mon, let's go take your things out of the car, Ameerah."

My team and I tagged behind Sister Tesneem and waited as she unlocked the car. Seconds later, Sister Tesneem turned around and handed me my dark purple gym bag.

"Here you go," she said. "Handle with care. Remember there's a trophy inside!"

"Yes, ma'am," I said with a grin. "Nobody is going to ruin this trophy. Nobody."

"Insha Allah," Sherine and the rest of the girls said collectively.

We all giggled. "Guys, guys," I said. "We have to keep practicing during the summer. At my house. Okay?"

"Of course!" said Sherine. "By the end of the summer, we'll be able to beat those Stallions right out of the court!"

"We'll be able to beat *everyone* out of the court!" quipped Aaliyah and Naailah.

"All in favor?" Reema held up her hand.

"Aye!" we chorused, slapping her a septuple high-five.

"A bit ambitious," Mina remarked with a shrug. "But we can make it work if we all work together."

I flipped my hair over my shoulder. "Yeah, that's true. We barely made the win today. My finishing shot had a giant risk of not making it."

"Alhamdulillah[7] the game resulted the way it did," Reema said, adjusting her purple glasses.

---

[7] All praise and thanks belong to God

A short moment after, a sleek red car pulled up by us at the curb. "Well, there's my ride," I announced. "Assalamu alaikum, guys! Assalamu alaikum, Sister Tesneem! Have a great summer!"

My coach waved at me with a big grin. "Later, Ameerah. Keep being yourself!"

"Wa alaikumussalam, Ameerah!" my friends called to me. "See you soon!"

I tossed my gym bag into the car first, then climbed inside. *My life can't get any better*, I thought with a smile to myself. And evidently, I was right. I'd ended my basketball season on a good note. I'd won a trophy. Our victory was celebrated at my favorite ice cream place. And I would spend my whole summer shooting hoops with all my friends. At this point, what could really go wrong?

Chapter 3
Hanaan

"Hey, Hanaan, wanna go out for ice cream?" my sister Rahima jauntily suggested as she entered my room one warm June afternoon.

"Uh, yeah! As if you even have to ask." I jumped up from the floor where I had been unsuccessfully trying to shape a complicated origami pattern.

"Yo, I can't believe you're still into origami," Rahima teased, watching me as I quickly set my papers aside and turned towards the door to join her. I passed by a bright blue frame on the wall and briefly smiled as I felt the familiar warm sensation that I had come to associate with the powerful words on the cream-colored paper behind the glass.

"What do you mean 'still'? I literally just got this origami book last week and I haven't even mastered all of my favorite patterns yet. And just because you don't have the patience to get through more than two folds doesn't mean that I don't."
I grinned knowingly at my sister who certainly did not enjoy crafting as much as I did. In fact, art had always been her worst subject which was still difficult for me to comprehend.

Rahima shook her head at me as she headed to her room to get herself ready. Her room was brightly lit with a ceiling light, a tall room lamp and a cute floral bedside lamp. She had a study desk at the front of her room, cluttered with notebooks, binders and sticky notes. Against her second wall, beside her closet, stood her vanity with a large mirror bordered by fancy scrolls and an endless number of drawers beneath. A variety of hijabs and pins covered the tabletop.

Her bed stood all the way in the back corner of her room, the blanket messily spread out on top, almost as an afterthought. I began feeling a perfectionist impulse to straighten out that blanket when Rahima's voice quickly drew my attention away.

"Plain navy blue or navy blue with swirls?" She held up two similar-looking hijabs, her head tilted to one side as she carefully examined both in the mirror.

I crossed my arms. "Seriously, Heema? It's kind of obvious that the swirly hijab matches better with the pattern on your dress."

"But that's why I have you, kiddo. I need someone to make fashion decisions for me." She tossed aside one of the hijabs and began wrapping the other around her head.

I always marveled at Rahima's skill for putting her hijabs on. She might not have been skilled at drawing or painting, but to me, the deftness of her fingers as they swiftly wrapped the cloth around her head was a true form of art. I loved watching as she tucked in the folds and positioned all her pins simply by the sense of touch. Whenever I tried to put a hijab on myself, I'd mess up everything, getting the ends of the scarf in all the wrong places and constantly being afraid that I'd poke myself with the pins. Which was why I always had Rahima do it for me whenever I wanted to wear one of her hijabs.

"So," Rahima said, patting down the front of her hijab and giving herself a quick look-over before turning to me. "Wanna go to Polar Point or to that other ice cream joint we went to last time?"

"Polar Point," I replied. "I'm definitely craving some strawberry cheesecake ice cream and I can't remember if the other ice cream store has it."

Rahima rolled her eyes. "You and your cheesecake ice cream. Okay, let's go." She reached into a pile of hijabs and her hand emerged with her car keys, a colorful keychain dangling below it.

"You still keep your keys there after what happened last time?" I asked incredulously, remembering the huge episode a week prior when I had helped her push aside her heavy vanity because she thought her keys had fallen behind it. It turned out that the keys had been under a pile of hijabs the whole time, which I couldn't help rubbing in every now and then.

"Chillax, Hanaan. It's not like I lost them again."

"And if you do lose them, you just expect me to find them again."

"Well, of course! I don't have Sherlock Holmes as a sister for nothing."

It was a long-standing family joke that I was somehow related to the fictional character Sherlock Holmes, a legendary detective who could crack any case. I had earned the title of "family detective" for my knack of figuring things out. It's not like I go hunting for mysteries to solve, though. I just observe things carefully, noticing what many others miss. My dad says it's because I don't talk all the time like my sister does. My mom says it's because I have a writer's eye and her genes.

Rahima says it's because I have her as a sister. Whatever the reason, I've always been grateful for my gift.

Yet this time, my powers of sniffing out clues and my ability to notice whenever something was up would fail me. As I slipped into the passenger seat of Rahima's car, I caught her eying me in a mysterious way, but I assumed it was still related to our conversation about her keys. She turned on the ignition, opening her mouth as if she were about to speak, then closed it quickly and turned away.

"Still can't admit that I'm right, huh?" I said, smirking. Rahima shook her head, apparently shaking away the thoughts that were lurking in her mind. "I always admit when you're right. What're you talking about?"

She raised her eyebrows in that funny way of hers and then placed her hand on my headrest as she slowly backed the car out of the driveway. As she turned her head back to the front, our eyes caught for a moment, and I saw a flash of something in her eyes. Was it nervousness? I gave her a confused look, but the next moment she said, "This heat is getting to me. Put the AC all the way up."

I turned the air conditioning knob, letting bursts of cool air circulate into the car. I was about to ask her if she wanted to tell me something when she launched into a hilarious story about one of her professors. Laughing until my sides ached, I forgot all about her mysterious glance. It wasn't until much later that I remembered something odd about that day, something that I hadn't realized. Throughout our conversation in the car, Rahima had been telling me funny stories and jokes, yet she hadn't laughed even once. Something had clearly been on her mind that day, but for once, I hadn't noticed. I, who noticed everything.

Chapter 4
Ameerah

"Another day done, another game won," I murmured to myself, stroking a metal, gold-colored cup the size of a papaya. My trophy. Printed on the base of the trophy were the words:

JUNIOR GIRLS' BASKETBALL
SPRING TOURNAMENT 2014
1ST PLACE AWARD

"Admiring that cup again, huh?" muttered a voice beside me.

I jumped. I'd hoped no one had heard me, until I remembered I was in the car with my three brothers, on the way home. Beside me sat my brother Ahmed, trying to pull off a cool image with his hair slicked into a mohawk and, like always, wearing no seatbelt. His bored face made me want to sock him in the arm. Could he be any less supportive?

"Yeah, Ahmed," I said. "And don't call it a cup. It's a trophy!"

He snorted. "Huh. Totally. Have you tried drinking from it?"

"No, but that's because it's not a cup!" I insisted.

"We'll see about that." Ahmed began to reach for my newly prized possession.

"Stop!" I squealed, yanking it out of his reach. "I don't want your grimy, nasty fingers all over my prize!"

Ahmed pulled his hand back, laughing. "Prize?" he scoffed. "That's fake gold. You know that, right?"

"Duh I know! But I don't ca-"

"Hey, hey, guys, chill. Cool it down," cut in Abdel-Hakeem from the wheel. "If I hear you guys argue one more time, I'm going to the print shop to have some posters made." He took one hand off the wheel to gesture headlines. "'New family wanted. Looking for willing takers of two squabblers. Must be separated at all times. Very good at housework, especially dishes.'"

Ali chuckled from the front passenger seat.

"I wasn't squabbling! He started it!" I jerked my thumb at Ahmed.

Ahmed hooted with laughter. "Me? What else can I say about someone looking at a trophy and talking to herself?"

"A '*congratulations*' would be nice," I returned. "Or even better, nothing at all."

"Congratulations for what?"

I felt like slapping that huge grin off his annoying face.

"You're just jealous," I finally huffed.

"Jealous of fake gold?" Ahmed giggled.

Abdel-Hakeem audibly sighed from the front seat. "Ali, what do you say we print 50 posters?"

"Nooo!" Ahmed and I shouted at the same time.

"That may not be enough," Ali responded. "We have to keep in mind a lot of people won't want them immediately, or at all."

"What else should we have on the poster? asked Abdel-Hakeem. "Hmm... note down 'both love to take out the trash.'" He glanced once at the rearview mirror and narrowed his eyes. "And one doesn't wear his seatbelt during car rides."

Ahmed quickly clicked on his seatbelt.

"Got it." Ali began typing on his phone.

"Aliii!" Ahmed and I whined. "Stoooppp!"

My two eldest brothers burst out laughing. "Like I said before, chill," Abdel-Hakeem chuckled. "I warned you not to argue anymore!"

"Yeah, but she —"Ahmed began.

"Ahmed, that's enough," Ali cut in firmly. "Ameerah worked really hard to get that trophy."

Ahmed closed his mouth and scowled. With a huff, he turned to look out of his window and said no more. I gazed through mine, too, hugging my trophy tightly to my chest, all the way home.

From the minute I started showing an interest in sports, Ahmed had made it his life's goal to discourage me. The idea of me playing basketball — and actually being good at it — was a joke to him, and he made sure I knew it. "I mean, come on, Ameerah," he would say with a smirk. "Face it. A midget like you is never going to master a slam-dunk."

"So what if I'm short?" I would retort. "At least I play sports. It's not like you do anything to get fit."

But if Ahmed was my critic, then Ali was my biggest cheer-leader. When I first told him that I wanted to train like an all-star athlete at age seven, he nodded and told me his workout schedule right away. He would bring me out with him whenever he went on one of his morning walks or late afternoon runs. If I ever com-plained about my legs getting tired, Ali would either stop where he was and allow me to rest for a bit, or since I was younger and much smaller back then, he would take me on a piggyback ride all the way home. Once he bought me a pair of rollerblades as an Eid present, and he spent the next few weeks teaching me how to use them. When he started playing soccer in eighth grade, I begged my parents to let me watch every single practice session and game. Before I ever picked up a soccer ball or joined a team myself, I knew every play, every move, every rule in the book. I played for a few years until I moved on to basketball. While Ahmed kept laughing at the thought of me trying to reach the hoop, Ali hyped me up until I joined my school's basketball team. It's because of him that, even though I barely reached a height of four-foot-six, I play just as well as any other girl on the court. Lately, our thing has been working on our health and nutrition together. We started a juice cleansing diet, an oily hair routine, oil pulling, and we were just getting into a green smoothie diet.

The point was, Ali was kind of my favorite brother. In that moment, I sure hoped Ahmed knew it.

My thoughts faded away as Abdel-Hakeem pulled into the driveway. "Alright, you losers, get out of my car," he ordered as he turned off the engine. "There's a whole lot of cleaning in here I gotta do."

"Not just in here," remarked Ali, escaping from the car before Abdel-Hakeem could punch him.

I pushed my door open and hurried out as fast as I could, desperate to get away from Ahmed. I reached the front door before anyone else and rammed my fist on it.

"Mama, Baba! Open up! I have something to show you!" I shouted.

Ali came up behind me, jingling the house keys in his hand. "Patience, princess," he chuckled.

I stepped aside to let him unlock the door, bouncing on my toes impatiently.

"Little show-off," Ahmed muttered.

The keys jingled, and Ali pushed the door open. "Ahmed, what did I say?"

"Yesss, Ali," Ahmed grunted, looking away and crossing his arms.

Ali nodded at him approvingly, then turned to me. "Ameerah, let me take your bag, and you can go inside, insha Allah."

I slipped my gym bag off my shoulder and handed it to him. "Thanks, Ali."

"No problem."

I wasn't looking Ahmed's way, but I could've sworn he rolled his eyes. "Hurry and get inside, Ameerah!" he said impatiently.

I turned to him. "Well, I would if you'd just be patient!"

"Says the one who couldn't wait for the door to open," Ahmed shot back. He gave me a little shove. "Move it!"

I'd already taken a step, but his shove toppled my balance. Panic flooded through me as my knees met the smooth hardwood. I caught myself just before my face hit the floor. Something hard pushed against my chest, knocking the breath out of me.

Behind me, I could hear Ahmed laughing. "Whoops!" he said. "That's... that's what happens to show-offs, I guess."

"Ahmed!" Ali cried incredulously. I heard him hurry over to me. I pushed myself up. Before me lay my new trophy, which sent a new flood of panic running through my veins. I snatched it up and quickly scanned it for any blemishes. *Does it have a scratch? Is it broken? Did it break anywhere?*

My heart suddenly stopped. Right there, on the front of my trophy, were tiny white criss-crossed marks. And criss-crossed marks meant blemishes. They hadn't been there before. Anger rose inside me, and I whipped around to face Ahmed, who'd stopped laughing, but seemed pleased with himself nevertheless.

"You think this is funny?" I snapped. I rose quickly to my feet and took quick, furious strides towards my brother. "You find this funny?" I repeated, thrusting the trophy into his surprised face. "Why don't you try and win a trophy for once, huh? Maybe something like *this* would better replace all those dirty dishes you stash in your room!"

Right at that moment my voice began to crack, and I stopped ranting. I wasn't about to burst out right in front of Ahmed. He stood frozen in the doorway, too shocked to speak, and Abdel-Hakeem had only just joined them. "Hey, what's all the fuss?" he asked. "Why the yelling? You alright, Ameerah?"

"Ask Ahmed!" I barked at him. Tightly gripping my trophy, I turned heel, yanked my gym bag off of Ali's shoulder, and stormed upstairs to my room. In my flurry of rage, I kicked my door open and chucked my gym bag across the room, where it landed in its assigned area under my window. Breathing heavily, I brought my trophy to my face again to survey the blemishes once more. The very sight of them only intensified my rage, and I could only let out that anger by tossing a swift kick to my door. At that moment, nothing was more satisfying than hearing the door slam shut.

Chapter 5
Hanaan

My sister Rahima always said that I was the best birthday present she ever had. I was born on her birthday, July 15th, when she turned ten years old. We were bonded together by our shared birthday immediately, and Rahima took her role as the older sister very seriously. She always wanted to be by my side, holding me close, helping me out. She is there in all of my baby pictures, never too far behind.

As for me, I always looked up to Rahima, always wanting to be like her, and luckily for me, she savored my affection for her instead of getting annoyed by it. She readily embraced the responsibility of being the older sister and treated me as a friend instead of as an irritation. I don't know if I would have been that charitable if our roles had been reversed.

My first word wasn't "Mama" or "Baba;" it was "Heema." Rahima bragged about this for years to our parents, to her friends, to anyone who would listen. As soon as I could walk, I would follow Rahima around everywhere, toddling along behind her on my little legs. I remember watching a video my dad took of the two of us playing outside when I was less than two years old. In the video, I followed Rahima around as she played in our sprinkler, helped my dad water our little vegetable garden, and jumped rope. But when she hopped onto her bicycle and started riding down the street, I started to cry, realizing that I would no longer be able to keep up with her. Good-natured and selfless as she was, my sister rode back and convinced my dad to attach a wheelbarrow to the back of her bike so she could carry me along.

And as the years went by, our relationship only grew stronger. When I had a nightmare, I would crawl into Rahima's bed. She would sleepily hold me close and my fears would diminish because I knew I had an older sister to protect me. Rahima always included me in whatever game she was playing, convincing her friends that I wasn't too little to understand. Her friends soon came to accept that a playdate with Rahima meant a playdate with Rahima and her little sister Hanaan. And Rahima's influence was so strong that they all came to love me almost as much as she did. One of the most special things about our relationship was the parallel between our names. When Rahima had found out she was going to have a sister, she was absolutely determined that I would be named Hanaan. Her favorite doll had been named Hanaan and had broken earlier that year, and I guess I was supposed to be some sort of reincarnation of her little playmate.

At first, my parents weren't very inclined to name me after a doll, and a broken doll at that. My mom wanted to call me something that rhymed with Rahima, like Karima or Saima because she thought it would be cute to have two daughters with similar names. My dad wanted to name me after his mother Minnah since Rahima was named after my mom's mom, Rahma. And they all argued about what to call me for months on end.

It wasn't until two weeks before I was born that they finally ended up with a compromise. While trying to convince my parents about the merits of the name "Hanaan," Rahima wrote up a list of very unique persuasive arguments. My parents nodded and smiled at her, waiting for her conclusion so they could remind her yet again that they were ultimately the ones who were going to decide on the name. I can picture the whole scenario in my head, even though I've only heard the story told by others.

Rahima had her hands clasped together as she passionately begged, "Pleeeeease. Hanaan is such a nice name! It looks so pretty when you write it and the meaning is just perfect. I looked it up in this Islamic names for baby girls book and it says that the name Hanaan means kind, compassionate, and tender-hearted. Wouldn't you love to have a baby daughter like that?"

And that's when my mom started a little because at that exact moment, I gave her a sharp kick from inside her tummy and she realized that the name Hanaan had the same meaning as the name Rahima. My mom was thrilled with the parallels between the two names and she thought that similar meanings were even better than names that rhymed. In fact, my mom got so obsessed with having names with parallel meanings that she was determined that my middle name should also match Rahima's middle name Imaan. It worked out that the name Amina was similar to the meaning of Imaan so I got to be named after my grandmother Minnah while sticking to my mom's new name theme.

And thus, I was named Hanaan Amina Imraan. Rahima was extremely proud that she had been the one to name me and always let others know the story behind my name. I had heard the story so many times that, once I was old enough to talk, I told people my own version of the tale. "So Heema and me are cinna- mons!" I would proclaim, attempting to explain that our names are synonyms.

When I got older, I began to realize that I took it for

granted that Rahima was homeschooled and was always around. Other than the times she attended various clubs and classes every week, she was at home, poring over books, solving problems in colorful notebooks, and surfing the web. I often sat beside her, wanting to learn like she did, wanting to be a "big kid."

My parents encouraged us to learn creatively and our house was as much a school as it was a home. We had a room filled with books, bookshelves lining the walls and a cozy sofa in the corner of the room for hours of uninterrupted reading. I learned how to read in that room, sitting beside Rahima as she read her favorite books out loud, doing voices for all the characters and adding in sound effects.

A large world map covered one wall in our living room. Every month, my mom would tack a tiny little flag on one of the countries on the map and that would be our "study zone" of the month. Rahima read countless articles online and passages from books in our library room. She would dress up in outfits from different cultures and even try her hand at making small traditional meals. To this day, I remember random details about countries all over the world because of this fun family activity.

We also had treasure hunts that my dad set up every few weeks. He would hang up clues and mysterious messages on a bulletin board in the kitchen and set two detective kits on the dining table. The contents of our kits varied depending on our mission. Sometimes there was a magnifying glass and binoculars. Other times there were scissors and tape. There was usually a stopwatch on the table, which meant that our mission was timed. Rahima and I would run around the house, searching for clues that would lead to the treasure. The clues would have carefully worded critical thinking problems that forced us to rack our minds for the solutions. Other times, they would be coded and would require us to solve multiplication tables or other math questions. But more often than working through the clues, I found it easier to veer off course in the middle of the hunt, looking for anything out of place in the house that could possibly hide our clues. While Rahima read and re-read the riddles, I would stake out various spots that were good for hiding things and often found the clues before Rahima did. My dad laughed when I noticed that the clock was a bit off-center, or the lamp was a bit wobbly. He had to start thinking harder when my sharp eyes made it impossible for him to hide clues in obvious parts of the house.

For a few hours every day, we would also sit down at our desks to fill in workbooks and work at our textbooks for the traditional subjects. But even then, I never thought of school in a negative light. I loved learning, and I loved having my sister right by my side. It wasn't until Rahima neared the end of high school that I began to see through a different perspective. That was when Rahima's studies were no longer characterized by fun activities and adventures. Even though I was very young, I could tell that her work wasn't a game anymore. She started taking many of her courses through an online school where she had teachers and guidance counselors and everything else in between.

In eleventh grade, she started taking classes at our local community college and twelfth grade was the big year she started applying to colleges. It was then that I began to realize that Rahima wouldn't always be at home anymore. She was growing up, spreading her wings, and I would be left at home, without her. Although my parents expressed a bit of sadness, I definitely took it the hardest.

Her first month at college was the toughest for me. Even though she still lived at home, she spent much of her time every day on campus, and I felt like she was never around. That year was also when my mom had just started working from home full time and my dad had lots of traveling to do for his job. Of course, they still spent time with me, and I did see Rahima every evening when she came home. But that didn't change the fact that our house felt emptier. Our wonderful homeschool environment no longer existed and I missed my sister terribly.

There was one thing that Rahima gave to me as a way to remember her by due to her absence. Rahima would always tell me Islamic stories of great heroes, fascinating miracles, and the deep meanings behind Qur'anic verses. One lesson that stuck with me the most out of everything that Rahima had taught me was a hadith[8] about the two lights. The hadith specifically referred to Surah Fatiha[9] and the last two ayahs[10] of Surah Baqarah[11] which both descended from the same door in Jannah. I loved this one especially because I always imagined that Rahima and I were two lights in the world. Two lights that no one would ever be able to separate.

---

[8] A saying or custom of the Prophet Muhammad (peace be upon him)

[9] First surah in the Qur'an

[10] Verses

[11] Second (and longest) surah in the Qur'an

Because I loved these verses so much, Rahima had these verses printed on a frame for me. And since then, that frame hung in my room, and I woke up to it every morning, with the reminder of Allah's words and my sister's love for me and our inseparable relationship.

Over time, I began to adjust to our new homeschool format. My parents hired tutors to teach me a few of the basic subjects and sent me to local homeschool groups and community activities to interact with other kids my age.

By the time Rahima was in her final year of college, I was quite comfortable with our routine. I spent as much time with Rahima as I wanted and everything was great in my little world…until I received the news that would change everything.

Chapter 6
Ameerah

It wasn't until the door was shut that I let the tears roll down my cheeks.

There. Just like that. My amazing day was ruined. All because of Ahmed! I could endure his teasing, but a ruined trophy? Not on my watch!

I stomped towards my bed and angrily sat down. That's when I spotted my trophy shelf. It stood proudly beside my bed, showing off all my achievements from the years before until now. My gaze switched to my sweaty hands, which held my newest trophy. Miserably, I fingered the scratches, cringing as I did so.

There's no way to fix this, I thought hopelessly. *It'll look like this forever.*

Fresh tears warmed up my face at the thought. Maybe I wouldn't have minded so much if this wasn't the last trophy I would win for the season. But it was, and I wouldn't be playing anymore until school started again! I leaned back into my pillows and continued to cry, feeling sorry for myself.

When my eyes had dried up, I climbed out of bed and stood before my trophy shelf. Most recent trophies always went on top of the shelf, and currently on top was the trophy I'd received last season. It was still perfect and shiny, the only flaw being the thin layer of dust it had collected. I picked up the trophy and turned it upside down to brush the dust off on my bed, then placed it beside the other trophies on the lower shelf. Reluctantly, I placed my new trophy on the top, then stood back to stare at it. If those marks weren't on the front of the trophy, I wouldn't have minded as much. But, unfortunately, there they were, square on the front. The blemish was hard to miss.

I sighed and lay down on my bed. My heart felt like it had been scraped on the front, too. I had waited hours and hours for that trophy to reach my shelf flawlessly, but no such luck. I rolled over and buried my face into my cold pillow.

A delicious aroma awakened me. With my eyes half-closed and still heavy with sleep, I sat up and sniffed, trying to recognize the smell. Sun-dried tomatoes and basil... pasta... cheese... all my favorite foods! *What's the occasion?* Rubbing the sleep out of my eyes, I climbed off my bed and took a look at myself in the full-length mirror that hung on my closet door. My half-ponytail hung loosely from my head, and stray dark brown curls sprang outwards. I was wearing a blue-and-white jersey with matching sweats, and white socks.

Blue-and-white jersey!

It all came back to me. I had won my last game of the season. That's why my mother was making my favorite foods! She always did after I won a game.

Last game of the season. That reminded me of my trophy. Ahmed's unsupportive attitude. I stared back at my newest trophy for a long minute. That's it. The damage was done and I couldn't continue stressing about it.

Well, Ahmed, I thought defiantly, *I don't care what you think. The rest of the family is celebrating my victory and there's nothing you can do about it.* My reflection in the mirror, as rumpled and messy as she was, placed her hands on her hips and smiled triumphantly.

"Ameerah!" called a voice from downstairs.

"Yeah?" I called back. I undid the lock and opened my door. At the base of the staircase, Ali stood holding the banister with one hand, and held his phone in the other. "Oh, hey, Ali," I said.

Ali glanced up and smiled when he saw me. "The princess has awakened," he commented.

Hearing my nickname "princess" put a smile on my face. My whole family called me "princess" because my name, Ameerah, was the Arabic word for princess. The only family member who didn't call me princess was Ahmed, who himself acted like some descendant of royalty.

"How did you know I was sleeping?" I asked, making my way down to meet him.

He smirked. "Because you look like you just woke up."

"Yeah, well, I was very tired. Of you," I joked.

"Mmhmm. As if you'd ever get tired of me." Ali ruffled my already-messy hair.

"Hey!" I giggled.

"Hey back," said Ali. "By the way, dinner is ready. Mama made your favorite food. That's what I came to tell you."

"I can tell," I said. "I could smell it from all the way up in my room."

Ali nodded. "Alright, then, I'll see you downstairs."

"Okay," I said, watching him leave. Suddenly, my stomach growled. Realizing how hungry I was, I hurried up to the bathroom to wash up. After washing my face, I headed down to the kitchen, wearing a dark purple tee with a pair of blue jeans, and I tied my dark brown curls into a fresh half-up pony.

The smell of cheese and pasta was overpowering my nostrils now. I couldn't wait to sink my teeth into all that yumminess.

"Heeeyy!" I chirped as I extravagantly entered the dining room. "The fun has finally arrived!"

My three brothers sat at the table in their assigned seats. At one end of the table, Ali sat texting, but slid his phone back into his pocket when I came. Abdel-Hakeem and Ahmed, sitting beside each other, were lost in conversation. Ahmed shot me a glance and opened his mouth as if he were about to say something, but seemed to think better of it and continued his conversation with Abdel-Hakeem.

In the kitchen, my parents were cleaning the countertops over a very interesting conversation. Mama, as always, was telling my father about drama that had occurred during work. My parents both worked at the hospital; Mama a pediatrician, and Baba a surgeon. They always came home with very interesting stories to tell. However, their stories came to a pause as I sauntered into the kitchen.

"Ammoura!" my dad chuckled. He walked over and ruffled my hair. "Did my little princess win a game *again?*"

I grinned. "Yes, Baba! You should have seen everything. I made the winning shot *last minute*. Or last second, you could say."

"No way, masha Allah[12]!" said Mama.

My father smiled tenderly. "Incredible."

---

[12]As God has willed

"The food is also incredible," Ahmed interrupted. "I mean, I haven't eaten it yet, but we'll see once we start eating."

Abdel-Hakeem kicked him under the table.

Mama laughed. "Oh yes. Ameerah dear, please help yourself. Your favorite!"

"Thank you, Mama!" I grinned widely.

My mother patted my shoulder. "Of course, baby. Also, there's orange chiffon cake for dessert."

I clapped. "Yaaay! I'm gonna have trouble cleaning my braces tonight."

"Yes, you will," Mama smiled. "Now, let's eat. Bismillah, everyone!"

I readily took my place at the table beside Abdel-Hakeem. He looked at me and winked. "Princess likes to let her brothers starve, eh?" he said.

I stuck out my tongue at him. "I'm here *now*."

"Yeah, like an eternity later," he said, then stuck a huge helping of salad into his mouth. I giggled and filled my plate with as much bean dip as it would accept.

After swallowing a forkful of his cheesy pasta, my father cleared his throat. "So, Ameerah, aren't you going to tell us all about the game?" he asked.

Out of the corner of my eye, I saw Ahmed roll his eyes. I grinned and decided to annoy him even more. "Oh, yes, Baba," I said passionately, sneaking a glance at Ahmed. "It was the most exciting experience of my life! In the first half, the game was so close. The lead kept switching between both teams and it was impossible to guess how it would end. And then, in the beginning of the second half, our team was in the lead. We started to feel pretty confident when all of a sudden Kamila from the other team somehow slipped through our defense and made two lay-ups in a row. And, oh my God, it was so nerve-wrecking! Reema started playing recklessly and fouled Wardah which got the other team another point. My heart was pounding in my chest the whole time and then I looked at the scoreboard and we were down by two points and there were only thirty seconds left! Finally, Sherine got to her senses and stole the ball from Kamila. But then she passed it to Aaliyah who wasn't expecting it at all and Aaliyah was literally *this close* to stepping out of the line. I called to her just in time and she passed me the ball, but when I turned to try and make the shot, every single player on the other team was right in front of the hoop, leaving no room for me to go and shoot. I stood there dribbling the ball in the middle of the court and the clock was ticking with only ten seconds to go. Everyone was sure this was it and I could tell the other team was ready to victory dance, but I was like, there's no way I'm gonna give up. So I casually walked up to the three-point line and right when there were three seconds left, I threw the ball up into the air and suddenly the whole audience went 'WHOA!' And then suddenly my team was all over me and screaming 'We won! We won!' It was literally the best thing ever." I finished my story with a huge grin on my face.

Throughout the story, I noticed Ahmed had been loudly crunching on tortilla chips, probably in attempt to drown my voice out.

The rest of my family, however, clapped enthusiastically.

"Nice. I wish I had been there," said Ali.

Abdel-Hakeem gave me a tight side hug. "Good job, princess."

"Yeah, good job for finally shutting up," Ahmed muttered.

My mother sighed. "I wish we'd arranged things better so we could have been there for your game," she said wistfully, and slid a glance at Abdel-Hakeem.

"I agree," my father said with a nod. "Last game of the season, too."

I frowned. None of my family had been able to attend my last game of the season. Unfortunately, something had to turn up for all of them. I shrugged, smiled again, and said, "Oh well, you know, there's always next season."

"And too bad you won't be on the team next season," Ahmed said smugly.

Abdel-Hakeem sucked in his breath and gave Ahmed another swift kick under the table.

"Ow!"

Ahmed's comment took me by surprise. "What?" I asked. "What do you mean?"

"Ahmed!" my mother scolded in a hushed tone. "I didn't mean to say anything until after dinner."

My brother shrugged and crunched on another tortilla chip.

I still wasn't getting any answers to the millions of questions beginning to fill up my mind. "Wait, what are you guys talking about? What's happening?"

My mother turned to me, her expression softening. She heaved a long sigh, then smiled. "Well, we have some good news for you, Ameerah. Next fall, you'll be homeschooling!"

Her words hit me like that basketball Sherine had once lobbed at my head from goofing around during practice. "What?" I managed to sputter.

My mother's smile widened. "Exciting, right? We've been researching homeschooling and it looks like a great option. You'll have a lot of flexibility to learn all the necessary subjects and emphasize on the ones you are interested in. So we're going to try it out, insha Allah."

Stunned, I made no reply. My bean dip was growing cold. I glanced at Abdel-Hakeem and Ali, but all they did was shrug and tip their heads at our parents.

I still didn't understand. *What about my real school? What's wrong with it?*

As if she had read my mind, my mother continued. "Here's why. Ayyub Academy has been a bit low on funds this year and can't find a full-time teacher for your grade, so it won't be offering seventh grade next year. And the school your brothers attend has reached its space limit for middle schoolers, so we added you to the waitlist, but the best option now seems to be homeschooling. We'll try it for a year, Ameerah, or until your school can find a full-time teacher. What do you say?"

What do I say? Oh, I had so many things to say. Like I wasn't liking the sound of any of this. "Bu-but what about Sherine, and everyone else? Where are they going?"

"I think Sherine's family has a bit more to worry about right now," my mother said. "They may… may not even be here in the fall."

"What?" I gasped. This 'good' news was getting worse by the second. My best friend, Sherine, not being here this fall? "Mama, what do you mean she won't be here this fall?"

"I'm sorry, Ameerah," my mother said. "Her family planned this last minute. They just received word that Sherine's grandmother is very ill, so their whole family is going back to be with her. They don't know how long they'll be there, or if they will even be back in the fall."

I couldn't think of how to react. I didn't know what to say. All too fast, my life had gone downhill. I placed my elbows on the table and laid my head in my hands, rubbing my temples, trying to process everything.

Abdel-Hakeem slid his arm around me and squeezed me close. "It's cool, princess. Maybe you'll end up liking homeschooling."

"Yeah. And you still have your other friends to hang out with," Ali added earnestly.

"Yup." Abdel-Hakeem squeezed my shoulder tightly. "It'll be okay."

I lifted my head and looked at my brothers. I didn't want to agree with them, but I was grateful to them for trying to make me feel better about the news.

"That a yes?" Abdel-Hakeem asked.

I smiled at him, even though deep inside, I wanted to scream. But I wasn't about to make a scene, especially considering the occasion behind my favorite dinner.

"There we go," my mother said, smiling. "Remember, it may just be for a year, okay love?"

I took a sip of my lemonade. "Yes, Mama."

The sound of Ali's phone suddenly buzzing startled me, and I choked on my lemonade. Excitedly, Ali hastened to fish the phone out of his pocket.

"Oh my God, yo, it's that dude, right?" Abdel-Hakeem asked Ali excitedly. He turned to me quickly, acknowledging my current situation. "You good, Ameerah?"

I coughed, my nose burning. "I'm good," I said hoarsely.

"Did you get it, son?" my dad was asking Ali.

"I'm hoping so," Ali replied, swiping and tapping the screen. He fell silent for a moment. A smile spread across his face, crinkling the corners of his eyes. "Guys, I got it! I start next Monday, insha Allah!"

Got what? I wondered, wiping my mouth.

My family rose into an uproar. Baba slapped Ali on the back. "Alhamdulillah!"

"Yaaay!" Mama squealed.

"Sweet!" Abdel-Hakeem clapped with enthusiasm.

Ahmed had food in his mouth, but he waved a chip in the air supportively.

"Got what?" I finally said in exasperation.

"My new job," Ali said absently as he slid his phone back into his pocket. Then he realized I was the one who had asked the question. "Oh, I didn't tell you?"

My curls bobbed up and down as I shook my head, and I let my bottom lip stick out. No one was telling me anything! Ali had a job now? And he didn't tell me? Did my opinion not matter or what?

Ali avoided my gaze. Was he feeling guilty for not telling me? I hoped he was.

"I'll be out Monday to Thursday every week, from 9 a.m. to 3 p.m.," Ali said.

"When will it end?" I asked.

"End of the summer. August 10."

I quickly did the math in my head. Two whole months?

I scrunched up my nose. There was no way I was going to survive three whole months of the summer without Ali! I pouted harder, if that was even a thing. "Well, that's... great," I finally said, crossing my arms. I didn't bother to watch Ali's reaction. Head bowed, I pretended to find interest in a piece of tortilla chip on the floor.

Beside me, Abdel-Hakeem cleared his throat loudly, as if acknowledging the awkward atmosphere. "Okay guys, guess what!" he exclaimed, flashing jazz hands. "I got some news for y'all. Can I say it now, Mama?"

I lifted my head a little and gave him a side glance. More news?

"Go ahead," Mama said with a smile.

Abdel-Hakeem flashed his forever perfect smile. Placing both of his huge hands on the table, he announced, "I am getting married!" emphasizing on each word for dramatic effect.

I now sat up straight. Now this was actually some good news! "Woah!" I said, clapping with the rest of my family.

"Mabrook[13]!" Ali, who didn't seem very surprised, cheered,

---

[13](Congratulations) blessed

slapping Abdel-Hakeem a high-five across the table.

"Dibs on taking your room!" Ahmed called out.

"You better," Ali said. "Then I can have a clean living space for once!"

"Oh dang. Y'all are too excited for me to move out," Abdel-Hakeem laughed. Turning to me, he said, "I think you'll like my fiancée, Ameerah. She's very friendly and has the best sense of humor."

I flashed him a smile—a real one, and reached out to give him a tight hug. "Congratulations."

Chapter 7
Hanaan

"Hanaan needs to hear it from you, Rahima. You've held it off too long already."

I had been reciting historical facts to myself when my mother's quiet voice interrupted my thoughts. I paused at the bottom step, adjusting the flowery bag that was draped around my shoulder.

Then, Rahima's voice drifted into the hall. "I know."

"She's gonna be upset if…" A cupboard door closed loudly, muffling the rest of my mom's words. I quickly walked through the hall and entered the kitchen where my mom sat on one of the dining table chairs, resting her arms on the table. She held a Qur'an open with her index finger as if she had been taking a brief pause from reading and wanted to keep her place. Rahima was standing by the counter, pouring herself a bowl of cereal. As I entered, both of them stopped talking abruptly, neither of them quite meeting my gaze.

I didn't want them to think that I had been listening to their conversation, so I took on a cheerful tone and said, "I'm heading out to Sister Jamilah's now."

My mom nodded. "Tell her I said salam." She looked at Rahima, whose back was still turned to me. I waited for a few more moments, but neither of them said anything more.

"Okay, so… assalamu alaikum," I said, walking towards the front door.

"Hanaan, wait." I stopped and turned when I heard

Rahima's voice, waiting to hear what she wanted to say. For some reason, my heart pounded fiercely and I couldn't figure out why Rahima's tone was making me nervous.

"Wanna go out for ice cream?"

"Um - what?" Whatever I had been expecting, that had definitely not been it.

"Ice cream. At Polar Point," my sister replied, as if we hadn't just gone out for ice cream yesterday, and we had never done so two days in a row before.

"I have to go to Sr. Jamilah's now. It's almost one." Why was Rahima being so weird? She knew that I did a few hours of school at our neighbor's house every day.

"Oh, right. I mean, yeah, I know, but after you get back?"

"Um, sure." I paused, waiting to see if she had something else to say. "Anything else?"

"Nope." And suddenly Rahima was her normal bubbly self again. "Give Hamza a huge hug from me and remind Jamilah about that email she was supposed to send me."

"Okay. Assalamu alaikum." This time, no one stopped me, so I unlatched the front door and stepped out of the house into the warm spring air.

Sr. Jamilah lived two blocks away from our house. She had moved into the neighborhood a few years ago when she had gotten married, and although she was older than Rahima, the two had become fast friends. Sr. Jamilah taught at our local Islamic school, which was very close to Rahima's university, so they often did the twenty-minute commute together. Then, a couple years later, Sr. Jamilah had Hamza, an adorable baby boy. Although she loved her teaching, she decided to take a break for a few years to look after Hamza. That was around the same time my mom started working longer hours for her job, so Sr. Jamilah offered to teach me a few subjects in her home. In exchange, I babysat Hamza for a few hours a day while she got things done around the house. We enjoyed each other's company so the arrangement suited us well.

I normally loved the walk to Sr. Jamilah's house, which allowed me to get a breath of fresh air and enjoy the surrounding nature. But today, I was preoccupied by the mysterious conversation in the kitchen.

Hanaan needs to hear it from you.

The words kept echoing in my mind, leaving an uncomfortable feeling in my stomach. What did I need to hear from Rahima? She was keeping something from me, something that my mom thought I should know. But Rahima never kept secrets from me. Never. When she came back from school, she would tell me all about her classes, her professors, her friends. She would tell me about the skateboarders doing tricks on the way to class or about different protestors filling up the quad. She would tell me when she was stressed out because all her midterms were coming up at once or one of her professors wasn't replying to her emails. And she would always take the time to ask about me. The two of us knew everything about each other. At least, that's what I'd always thought.

I racked my brain, grasping at any possible clues, trying to figure out when exactly Rahima had started acting strangely. Come to think of it, she hadn't just been acting weird for a few days. Over the past few months, I had noticed that Rahima seemed excited all the time, forever giddy with anticipation. I'd thought that it had been because of her upcoming graduation and the fact that she had finally finished all her applications to graduate school. And she had never denied it whenever I brought it up.

The past two weeks, though, had been especially strange. Rahima would be on the verge of saying something to me, but would change her mind at the last moment and bring up some random story about school. I had begun to suspect that something was going on, but my mom's words today had confirmed it.

Those thoughts whirled around in my brain as I walked up the front steps of Sr. Jamilah's apartment building, barely watching where I was going. The door opened as soon as I rang the doorbell. Sr. Jamilah looked frazzled. Her hair was tied back in a loose bun with hair escaping every which way. She was wearing a pair of wrinkled pajama pants and a t-shirt with mysterious stains on it. In her arms was a squirming toddler who was wearing nothing more than a diaper.

The sight threw all thoughts about Rahima out of my mind. Sr. Jamilah usually wanted everything neat and orderly. It was definitely not like her to still be in her pajamas, holding an undressed Hamza.

"Assalamu alaikum, Hanaan," she greeted breathlessly, ushering me into the house and nearly dropping Hamza into my arms. "As you can see, my day has not exactly started out well."

I replied to her salam, kicked off my shoes, and gave Hamza a little tickle under the chin. The normally cheerful toddler pushed my hand away and began to whine.

"He's not feeling very well," Sr. Jamilah explained, passing her hand over her hair as she led me into the living room.

"He threw up two times last night, so neither of us got much sleep. I just gave him a bath, so he should start feeling sleepy soon. As soon as I get him to sleep, we can start studying. Okay?"

"Sure," I replied. I took another look at her shirt, beginning to realize what the stains were. "Actually, why don't I put him to sleep? Then you can clean yourself up and stuff." I glanced down at Hamza, whose eyes looked droopy. His head was resting on my shoulder.

Sr. Jamilah shot me a grateful look and chuckled. "Yeah, I must look like a mess."

"No, I don't mean…"

But she laughed again and I knew she hadn't been offended. Soon enough, I was whisked off to Hamza's bedroom while Sr. Jamilah went to take a quick shower.

A few hours later, Hamza was napping soundly while Sr. Jamilah and I lounged in the living room, talking about World War II over a snack of brownies. We always left history for last because it was what I enjoyed the most. Sr. Jamilah always made learning history an adventure, giving me lots of fun projects and activities that I always looked forward to. Sometimes I would act out the role of a historical figure, making my own costumes and reciting famous speeches. Other times, I would put together three-dimensional posters to recreate famous sculptures and scenes. Best of all, she had me read lots of historical fiction related to each period we covered. I had a feeling that going all out with me was her way of filling the void of not teaching at school.

"Here." Sr. Jamilah handed me two books she had just

picked out from the shelf. "Start reading these and we can talk about them in a few days." I took the books and carefully placed them in my bag. Sr. Jamilah usually didn't lend out her books to many people, but I was an exception, mostly because we both treated books like they were living creatures, keeping them clean and safe from creases. As I put away my remaining books and pencils, she packed a few brownies inside a plastic container for me to take home to my family.

"I know Rahima's sweet tooth will appreciate these," she said, grinning.

"Rahima could eat these brownies all day," I affirmed. "It's a good thing I got to eat some already. She'll probably finish the rest of these within the hour."

Sr. Jamilah laughed. "Speaking of Rahima, I just remembered that I was supposed to email her about reserving the event hall at Masjid Nurayn. She's in love with the masjid."

"Oh yeah, she told me to remind you to email her."

"I'll do it today, insha Allah. So how's she doing?"

Her question immediately resurfaced my thoughts from earlier that afternoon.

"She's been acting weird lately," I blurted without thinking.

"Well, of course," was her astonishing response. "Every bride has jitters. And especially since all the wedding planning is happening last minute. Rahima has a lot on her mind…" Sr. Jamilah stopped abruptly when she saw the expression on my face. "Are you okay, Hanaan?"

I couldn't reply. I had been stunned into silence by her words. Bride? Wedding? What on earth was Sr. Jamilah saying?

"I h-have to go," I stuttered, standing up. My legs felt wobbly, like the very ground I was standing on had been shaken.

"Wait, Hanaan…" But I was already standing at the front door, struggling to turn the lock. "Are you sure you're okay?" Sr. Jamilah now looked concerned.

"Yes…no…I have to go. Thanks for the brownies. Assalamu alaikum." I stumbled out of her apartment and walked blindly towards home.

I don't know how I made it, but eventually I reached our tall blue house, pushed open the front door and hurried up the stairs to my room. Rahima was waiting for me in the hall.

"Hey, Hanaan," she greeted me cheerfully. "Ready for some ice cream?"

Ignoring her question, I glared at her, my voice shaking with anger.

"Is it true?" I demanded.

"Is… wait, what?" Rahima sputtered.

"Does 'wedding' ring any bells?"

The expression on her face told me all I needed to know, but I wanted to hear her say it. "So it's true?"

Rahima took a deep breath. "Yes, I'm getting married," she said.

"And of course you didn't think to tell me," I spat. "I'm only your sister."

"Hanaan, I was going to tell you…" But I didn't wait to hear what she had to say. I pushed past her, stormed into my room and slammed the door shut.

Chapter 8
Ameerah

"Ahmed! Ameerah! Wake up!"

I bolted upright, surprised that my mom's voice was waking me up instead of my alarm clock. I took a glance to the right, seeing that the clock read 7:55 am, five minutes before it would go off.

"Coming!" I called back, tossing off my blanket and walking into the hallway for the bathroom. Yawning, I fumbled around for the light switch and flipped it up. Through my half-lidded eyes, I could just barely make out the rat's nest my hair had turned into overnight.

As I scrubbed the sleep out of my face with cold water, my gaze cleared and focused on the toothbrush holder. Ahmed's green and blue Leonardo Teenage Mutant Ninja Turtles toothbrush was the first one I noticed, bristles facing every which way. I turned off the tap and began patting my face dry with a soft towel, wondering how Ahmed had gotten his toothbrush to look that way. What did he do, shove it down the garbage disposal? Or did it take that much more effort to get the gunk out of his teeth?

As if on cue, Ahmed walked into the bathroom just then. "Hurry up, I need to pee," he said drowsily.

I hung the towel back on its rod and stuck out my tongue at him before leaving. I was still a little annoyed at him for what he'd done yesterday, especially since he hadn't really said he was sorry. Once I'd stepped out of the bathroom, my gaze landed on the door leading to Ahmed and Ali's room. It was open, but only because

Ahmed wasn't inside. Then I noticed Abdel-Hakeem's room, which was also open and unoccupied. *Where's he at?*

The sunlight from the arched window above our front door seeped into our top floor, creating a pretty row of sunny bands on the hardwood. I headed downstairs, raising my left eyebrow questioningly when I heard the vacuum turn on from a few rooms away.

Oh my God, is Mama really doing a deep-clean right now? That's for Sunday. Oh, wait. It is Sunday. Since summer started, I hadn't been keeping track of the days. With a laugh, I let my hand slide off the banister and stepped onto the bottom floor. Not all the shoes were on the shoe rack this morning. Ahmed's blue and green sandals were on the floor, one of them upside down. And besides my sneakers and Mama's sandals, everyone else's shoes were missing. Baba and my oldest brothers were out somewhere. *What are they up to?*

Curious, I turned and walked into a living room that looked like someone had been trying to look for misplaced car keys. The sofa had been gutted of its cushions, the lamp was on the right side of the fireplace instead of the left, and there was a new elegant succulent on a side table instead of the usual tissue box. *Wow, with the way Mama's cleaning today, you'd think we were having guests.*

I didn't see anybody so far, but I knew I wanted to eat something. Hunger overpowering my curiosity, I prepared myself a yummy tomato sandwich and a glass of strawberry lemonade.

As I took a bite of my sandwich, my nose wrinkled up. It didn't taste like a tomato sandwich. There was a gross tinge to it. "Did the mayonnaise go bad?" I asked myself. I held the sandwich to my nose and sniffed. It smelled like fresh white bread and mayonnaise. It didn't smell bad.

"That's weird," I said, setting the sandwich back onto my plate. As I did so, the nasty smell filled my nostrils again. Confused, I sniffed the air. *Or maybe my sandwiches just are as nasty as Sherine and the rest say they are...*

The entire kitchen smelled like Clorox and oranges. "Well, that explains it," I said, turning to walk out of the kitchen. "I'm not gonna eat in here." Mama only broke out the orange-scented Clorox when she was doing *deep*, deep cleaning. *But why?*

As I headed out, I noticed five boxes of tortellini pasta laid out on the counter, among a bunch of vegetables and spices. Even more tortellini than it took to prepare dinner for the whole family. "Whaaat is going on?" I asked to no one in particular. I sat down at the dining table to finish my breakfast.

Thoughts of Sherine popped back into my mind as I took another bite of my sandwich. I remembered how she was leaving and that I couldn't see her all summer. *If I could only see her today for the last time right before she —*

The whine of the vacuum from a few rooms away drowned out my thoughts, along with any and all other sounds. Where was Mama?

"Maamaa!" I yelled over the vacuum. "Where are you?" I heard the vacuum pause for a moment, and then switch off.

"Ameerah?" Mama called. "Come here; I'm in the guest room."

Stuffing the rest of my sandwich in my mouth, I hurried towards the guest room and found Mama wrapping the power cord back onto the vacuum. She glanced up as I entered. "Good morning, Ameerah," she said, smiling.

I walked over to give her a hug. "Good morning, Mama. What's going on?"

"Sunday cleaning." Mama stood up, squeezed me back, then rolled the vacuum out into the hallway and into the cleaning supply closet. "You know we clean every Sunday."

"No, I know that, but I mean the kitchen," I said, following her. "Why are you making so much food? And why does the living room look like Baba lost his car keys? And where are Abdel-Hakeem and Ali?"

Mama laughed. "We're having visitors — special visitors. Your brothers went out for grocery shopping."

Visitors; I knew it! "Visitors? Who are they?" I followed her into the living room and watched her puff up the cushions. *Maybe it's Sherine!*

Mama tossed me a cushion. "Some special friends. You'll see. Now, enough questions. Help me clean up this living room. Is Ahmed awake?"

I caught the cushion. "Yes, Mama. He's in the bathroom."

"Good. Also, I'm going to have you help Baba fix the garden a little after this. Right now he's at work doing the morning shift because he needs to be here in the evening. He'll come back home today around two, so that should give us enough time."

"Fix the garden?" I fluffed the cushion up. "Is it broken?"

Mama heaved a sigh. "Oh my Lord, Ameerah."

I giggled. "What?"

She said nothing in response, but smiled.

"When are the guests coming?" I picked up another

cushion to fluff.

"Around 5:30."

"When do they leave?"

Mama shrugged. "We'll see."

Huh? I gave my mother a questioning look, but she disregarded it with a little smirk and pushed all the cushions back into place, motioning for me to do the same. For a moment, an uncomfortable feeling crept over me, telling me that my mom was hiding things from me again. I opened my mouth, considering confronting her about exactly what was going on, but she seemed to be in a good mood, and I wasn't quite in the mood either to argue, so I pushed the cushion back into the couch. And I had a teeny bit of hope within me that maybe these mysterious guests were Sherine's family, coming over for one last time before they left the country. For the rest of the day, I worked with Ahmed and my dad to straighten up the lawn and the garden, while Abdel-Hakeem helped my mom with the cooking, and Ali cleaned the rooms. When the house was finally spotless, we were left with about an hour left until the visitors arrived, so I took a shower and changed into my favorite outfit. I pulled my hair into a half-pony and snapped two silver hair clips on each side of my head.

"Changing into favorite everything just for Sherine!" I sang to myself.

Mama had told me to clean my room, so I spent the rest of my time throwing and stuffing things here and there. I tossed my basketball into my closet, kicked my gym bag to its assigned area under the window, and hastily straightened the purple covers on my bed.

Outside, I heard a car door slam, making me jump. *Sherine! She's here!* I hurried out of my room and nearly slid down the stairs. All my brothers were already by the base of the staircase, wearing their best shirts. Not formal dress shirts, but just the shirts they hadn't somehow ruined. They all stood in the hallway, and I joined them. Ali, wearing a black T-shirt and blue jeans, stood with his phone in his hands, typing rapidly. *Probably all that job stuff,* I thought, feeling a little prickle of resentment all over again.

To get my mind off Ali, I snuck a quick glance at Abdel-Hakeem. His glossy brown hair was neatly parted to one side. He looked very handsome in his white-and-blue plaid, pulled over a white T-shirt.

"Well, look at *you*," I teased, glancing at Ali as I did. I wanted to see if he'd notice that I was talking to my other brothers first and not him. "Who are you dressing up for?"

Grinning, Abdel-Hakeem tapped me on the nose. "Shhhh, princess!"

"Calling me princess won't make me stop," I returned, smirking. "Now really, why are you dressed all fancy?"

At that, Ali glanced up from his phone. "Why do you think?" he asked, the corner of his mouth twitching.

He and Abdel-Hakeem were both looking at me now with little grins on their faces, which I could tell they were trying to hide. I shot a glance at Ahmed for any potential assistance, but he was still trying to get his Teenage Mutant Ninja Turtles shirt to cover his belly. Baffled, I looked back at my two eldest brothers, questions on my face.

Ali finally broke it to me. "His special person is coming."

"Special person?" I asked. "What special person?"

Abdel-Hakeem wiggled his eyebrows at me, and that was when I realized. *His* special person. His special person! It must be his *bride!* "Woah," I said. *But... I thought it was gonna be a friend...*

Just as I said that, the doorbell rang.

My mother, dressed in a black abaya and a white hijab, hurried to the door. With her hand on the doorknob, she inspected us quickly. "Ahmed, can you please change into a different—oh, never mind, it's too late now." She opened the door. "Assalamu alaikum!" she greeted the visitors warmly. "Please, come in. Remove your shoes inside; it's alright."

I watched an unfamiliar man walk inside to shake hands and slap backs with my father. My brothers walked over to shake hands as well, leaving me beside the stairs to stare at everyone.

A young woman, tall and very pretty, stepped inside the house after that. I guessed she was the bride since she was the only person in the unfamiliar crowd who looked to be of marriageable age. She was a very smiley person indeed. Maybe it was just because Abdel-Hakeem was in the room, but her grin never faded for a minute. Her light brown eyes twinkled as if she shared a secret joke with everyone, and I could see already what Abdel-Hakeem had meant by "best sense of humor." She did look like a very fun person.

Right behind the bride stood a shorter girl, dressed in a pink T-shirt and a long white skirt. I watched her carefully take off her black flats and place them neatly beside each other next to the door. *Who is she?*

I heard my mother squeal with joy over the younger girl.

"Aww, look at you! And what's your name, dear?"

If the girl had answered, I didn't catch it. I studied my nails, my annoyance growing because my mother had deceived me. I had been so sure the visitors were going to be Sherine's family! I didn't know that girl. What was my mother thinking when she said a friend was coming over? And hearing her talk to the girl as if we'd known her for years only added to my annoyance.

"Oh, you are so adorable, masha Allah!" she was saying. "Have you met my daughter Ameerah? She should be around your age. Oh, this is so perfect! You two can be best friends!"

I held back a snort. Best friends? *Excuse me, Mama! You know I don't want to hear those words right now.* Annoyed, I ran my tongue over my braces.

"Ameerah?" my mother then called. "Where is she?"

Reluctantly, I sauntered out of the shadows, my hands shoved into my pockets. All the pairs of eyes focused on me. "Assalamu alaikum," I said nonchalantly.

"Ah!" My mother smiled. "This is my daughter, Ameerah," she told the other mom. "Ameerah, this is Aunty Nusaybah."

I shook the lady's hand. "Assalamu alaikum," I said again.

"Wa alaikumussalam, Ameerah!" said the lady, squeezing my hand tightly. "It's so good to finally meet you. I know Rahima is excited to get to know you, too." She turned to the older girl.

"Of course!" Rahima said, giving me a squeeze on the shoulder. "Abdel-Hakeem has told me so much about you."

"Come to the dining room for some food, insha Allah," said my mother, leading everyone to the dining room we had beautifully prepared with varieties of food. All the boys and men headed to the dining table to take their food, while the ladies sat in the living room to talk. I leaned back into our recliner, listening to the conversation.

It had to be the most boring conversation I'd ever heard. The mothers talked about their childhood, how they got married, and their jobs. I could have sworn I was falling asleep in that recliner.

Then my mom said, "Oh! You know I mentioned before that we are starting to homeschool Ameerah this coming fall. Perhaps Hanaan could give her some advice on how to start, yes?"

I sat up in the recliner and studied the girl they called Hanaan. She sat beside her mother with her hands clasped in her lap and her eyes downcast. She didn't seem like one to talk. *Yeah, because she's a homeschooler,* I thought. *I don't want to be like that.*

Hanaan looked at my mother, expressionless. Then it hit me. I'd seen this girl before, several times at the masjid, hanging out with older girls, and could always be seen with her older sister. I'd never heard her speak a word before. And I didn't expect her to say one now. I leaned back in the recliner, even lower this time. *Oh, this is gonna be a long day.*

After the men had all taken their food, it was our turn. They brought their plates and cups to the living room to eat, and the ladies headed for the table, still talking their heads off. I dragged my feet behind me at the back of the group, studying Hanaan's long black braid.

"Please, everyone sit down," my mother said. Aunty Nusaybah and her girls sat down at the table, and I couldn't help cringing when I saw Hanaan take my unofficially assigned seat.

"Would you all like some lemonade? Tea, perhaps? Or maybe some milk?" my mother asked. "My Ameerah here loves to drink milk by itself," she added with a laugh.

I wanted to roll my eyes. *If not by itself, then with what? Orange juice?*

Rahima laughed, as well. "That's totally normal!" she said. "My sister eats tuna fish straight out of the can!"

"Well now, don't our daughters sound just like little kittens," Aunty Nusaybah joked.

Hanaan shot a look at her mother. She obviously did not appreciate the joke, or even the idea of being associated with me. I poured lemonade for Rahima and Hanaan, tea for the mothers, and milk for myself, then grudgingly took Ali's seat at the end of the table. Over our meal of tacos, bean dip, and cheesy tortellini, I kept sneaking glances at Hanaan, who ate rather primly but with a stormy expression on her face. She chewed on one piece of tortellini at a time, and after every tiny bite of her taco she would cover her mouth with her napkin.

What's her problem? I thought. *You'd think she'd be happy her sister's getting married.* At least I had a reason to be mad. No, not a reason. Several reasons. My family told me nothing of their new plans, which led me to not being able to see my best friend and worrying like a fish out of water about how to spend my summer. I stabbed three pieces of pasta with my fork and stuffed them into my mouth.

After the meal, the mothers and Rahima talked nonstop. "I know you and Abdel-Hakeem talked about when the wedding will happen," my mom said, addressing Rahima. "But is the date finalized or are you still working on that?"

"We'd like to have at least a week to get settled into our new home before Ramadan starts," Rahima responded. "So we were thinking the weekend of the 21st."

"And the 21st is a Friday or Saturday?" My mom had taken out her phone and was awkwardly scrolling down her screen while holding her fork between her fingers.

"It is a Saturday," Rahima's mom confirmed, holding up her own phone. It seemed she had accessed her calendar more quickly.

"Yup, I found it, too," my mom said triumphantly, as she held up her phone next to Aunty Nusaybah's. I watched in exasperation as they both compared their phone calendars.

"They're both exactly the same," I muttered to myself, wishing they would start talking about something else, but the next moment they were talking about wedding venues.

"Remember that huge Eid party we had two years ago?"

My mom let out an excited squeal. "You know, that is exactly what I was thinking, too! What was the place called? The Tres Belle Hotel?"

"Yes, yes," Aunty Nusaybah was nodding her head vigorously. "I've been telling Rahima that the best thing would be to get a reservation there, if possible. I know it may be difficult to reserve a room with such short notice, but we have contacts, isn't that right, Rahima?"

"My friend Jamilah was getting me into contact with the reservation coordinators at Masjid Nurayn," Rahima replied.

Her mom shot her a disappointed look. "Rahima, I thought you agreed that the hotel would be the best suited venue for the wedding."

A hint of a shadow passed Rahima's face. Or maybe I just imagined it, because the next moment, she was laughing. "I was just going to say that Jamilah gave me information about affordable wedding planners, so insha Allah, we can spend less time on planning for the wedding and more time setting up our new home."

Both moms gave little squeals of delight and I fought back a groan. This was turning out to becoming the dullest conversation ever, and I was literally dying of boredom. I would do anything to no longer have to hear about that darn wedding. *Maybe if I get her attention somehow, she'll remember I'm here and stop talking about boring wedding plans.* I stood up from the table, seized the milk carton, and put it back in the fridge. Thankfully, Mama noticed.

"Oh, Ameerah," she said, "why don't you take Hanaan up to your room so you two can get to know each other better?"

I curled my toes on the hardwood to contain the anger welling up inside me. Well, *that* didn't work out the way I expected! Take that girl to my room? *NO, Mama! I do NOT want to talk with this girl. So I am NOT taking her to my room!* I wanted to punch the fridge, but instead I mustered a half-smile and managed to say, "Yeah. Sure."

I watched Hanaan edge out of my chair and hesitantly walk towards me. The girl strode over the freshly cleaned hardwood floor. As she came closer, I looked her over. She raised her sharp brown eyes to me and tucked a stray strand of hair behind her ear.

Well, Ameerah, I told myself, *if this is what you have to deal with, give it your best shot.* With a flip of my curls, I turned and marched up the staircase, not caring to check if she was close behind.

Chapter 9
Hanaan

I could tell Ameerah had not wanted to take me to her room, but what else could she do with her mom asking her in front of everyone? I followed her up the winding staircase, the kind that always makes me dizzy. I was hating everything about this house and its inhabitants already.

Ameerah was walking fast, as if daring me to catch up, but I didn't take the bait. I walked as slowly as I could without drawing attention from everyone else. She didn't want to play this game? Well, great, because neither did I. She could wait for me at the top of the stairs; I was going to take as long as I wanted.

But Ameerah didn't turn around. She strode through the hallway and opened the first door a bit roughly. She wordlessly entered the room and didn't even motion for me to follow her. I stepped into her room behind her and took a few moments to look around. The room looked like it had been very messy but hastily cleaned up. The walls were painted a dark shade of purple, and a twin bed sat in the center of the room. The bed was messily made, the corners of the purple blanket uneven and a pillow sitting lopsided atop it. A dartboard hung on the wall across from the bed. Beneath the large window on the side of the room was a gym bag with clothes spilling out of it. Shelves lined the walls, but unlike my shelves, these were covered with trophies and medals rather than books. In fact, the shelves were the only things in the room that were spotlessly clean.

As I looked around for her nonexistent desk, Ameerah

kicked her gym bag under her bed and deliberately turned one of her trophies around so that the writing was no longer facing me. She looked almost angry, and I couldn't tell whether it was directed at me or at something else. Either way, I was annoyed. She didn't have to hide her trophies from me. I didn't even care what was written on them or what they were for.

I watched as she pulled over a foldable chair from her closet and dropped herself down on it, pushing strands of her curly brown hair from her face, still refusing to meet my gaze. I had had a few encounters with Ameerah at our local masjid before and had seen her there often, but this was the first time we were sitting together alone. From what I had seen, Ameerah was the type of girl who liked to be at the center of things. She always had a bunch of girls around her, chatting and giggling, particularly with her friend Sherine. Around those girls, she always talked loudly and passionately, so it was a little surprising to see her so tight-lipped and uninterested right now.

"So…" Ameerah drew in a breath and motioned for me to sit on her bed. It looked like she was finally deciding to play the hostess. I sat stiffly on the edge of the bed, my hands folded in my lap and my feet planted firmly on the carpet. "What kind of stuff do you like to do?"

"Umm." I paused. I didn't feel like telling this girl who was basically a stranger about Fajr's Shadow or about my latest writings. "I like to read," I said finally.

"Oh." She obviously didn't know what to say to this.

"What about you?" I asked. It seemed like the right thing to say.

"Sports," she responded immediately, evidently having no scruples about sharing her passions with me.

"Oh," I said. That explained the trophies and medals. "Are you on a team?"

For some reason, this question seemed to upset Ameerah and she was momentarily silent. "Used to be."

"Oh," I said again.

"What about you? You on a team—I mean, club for reading? A book club?"

"Well, in the fall, I was in a book club at the library. And last summer, I kind of joined an informal book club with my sister and her friends." At the mention of Rahima, my voice faded away as I remembered why we were at Ameerah's house. My thoughts went back to a few days ago when I had first found out that Rahima was getting married. It was as if everything had come crashing down that day. One day, Rahima and I had been the closest of sisters, sharing everything with each other and the next, I found out that she was getting married and moving out. But the worst part was that she had kept all this a secret from me and I found out all this from our neighbor.

I remembered coming home from Sr. Jamilah's house and staying secluded in my room, ignoring Rahima's attempts to speak with me. When I had finally come downstairs to eat dinner with my family, I refused to talk to my sister or to even look at her. After we ate, my mom who had evidently realized that I had found something out and was keeping my distance from Rahima, told me all the details in an excited tone.

"A wedding, Hanaan! It's going to be so much fun, insha

Allah. And, of course, the Sallehs are such a wonderful family."

"The Sallehs?"

"Yeah…oh, Hanaan! Didn't you know Rahima is going to marry Abdel-Hakeem, the oldest of the Salleh children?"

"No, how was I supposed to know? No one bothered to tell me."

"Hanaan," my mom had said quietly, dropping her cheerful front. "Rahima was worried about you. She knew you would be upset that she's moving out and she wanted to spare you a bit of that until everything was all settled and certain."

"But why is she moving out? It's not fair." My voice cracked a bit, but I was determined not to break down.

"Hanaan, the Salleh family are such wonderful people, and we've gotten along so well with them over the past few months. You'll see once you get to know them better how friendly and sincere they are. And Abdel-Hakeem is basically everything Rahima ever wanted in a guy. He's nothing like that other kid who came over last winter. Remember the one whose mom kept praising him? He just kept nodding to everything she said and reaching for more food."

I remembered exactly what she was talking about, but refused to be sidetracked. "So Rahima's found her dream guy, huh?"

My mom smiled in an over-enthusiastic way. "Yes, she did. And he lives in the same city so she's only going to be a ten-minute drive away. It's all going to be so convenient and perfect, insha Allah!"

I frowned. I clearly had a different idea of what was perfect than my mom did. For me, perfect would be Rahima staying home with me where she belonged instead of gallivanting across town with a guy who had no business taking her away. And a ten-minute drive? For someone who had lived in the same room or across the hall from Rahima my whole life, that distance seemed millions of miles long.

"But Hanaan," my mom said curiously. "If Rahima didn't tell you, then how did you find out?"

"Sr. Jamilah," I muttered.

"Ohh." A look of understanding flooded my mom's face. Suddenly, from the corner of my eye, I could see Rahima standing in the hallway, leaning on the wall with a somewhat regretful look on her face. She was twisting a strand of hair around her finger and staring a bit too hard at a spot on the ground. Having no room for pity for her, I declared, "Well, I don't care that she's moving away. If she can't face up to me before my tutor has to tell me that my sister is getting married, then she can marry an eskimo and move to Alaska for all I care." And I angrily left the room, leaving my mom and sister alone in stony silence.

"Um, what else do you like to do?" Ameerah's voice broke me out of my thoughts.

I blinked. "Sorry?"

"Do you like to do anything else besides reading?"

"Yeah." I didn't elaborate. I could tell she already thought I was a nerd, and I wasn't going to feed her stereotypes with more of my hobbies. "What about you? Do you like to read?"

Ameerah shook her head. "Nah, not really."

"Oh," I said, even though I had already expected that answer. I didn't know what else to say and this situation was frustrating me. Because of my sister's decision to marry into the Salleh family, I was stuck hanging out with…oh my God! My future sister-in-law?! My eyes widened as I suddenly realized that this girl who I had nothing in common with was about to become part of my family. I was horrified at the thought. Up until now, our parents had been the only ones to meet up with Rahima and Abdel-Hakeem. But now that there was a wedding on the horizon, were our families going to meet up regularly from now on? Would we be stuck together like this for the rest of the summer? For the rest of our lives?

Ameerah seemed to be reading my thoughts because the next thing she said was, "So…looks like we got ourselves a wedding coming up."

"Looks like."

"Have you been to a wedding before?"

"Yeah, a few times." I recalled the wedding I had attended last summer. Rahima's friend Zaynab was getting married and she had teased Rahima that she was next. I had laughed because I had thought it was just a joke, but thinking back, I realized how that conversation was now coming true.

"I've never been to a wedding before. Never really thought about it before actually. Do you like weddings?" Ameerah was now looking straight at me, waiting for my answer.

"Depends on who's getting married," I said, slowly and deliberately. I wondered if she would take that as an insult to her brother, and then I found myself hoping that she would. But she didn't seem to care or maybe she didn't realize what I was trying to imply because the next moment she turned her head towards the wall behind her and said, "Wanna throw some darts?"

I had never been this close to a dartboard before, forget actually throwing darts, but I wasn't going to show this girl any signs of weakness. "Sure."

Ameerah immediately stood up and grabbed a bunch of darts from the top of her chest of drawers. She threw a few darts to show me how and then removed them from the board. When she handed me one, I leaned back, aimed as sharply as I could, and letting all my built-up emotions flow through my arm, I threw the dart as hard as I could. It landed with a satisfying thud on the board, and I couldn't help myself from grinning. Ameerah and I were two opposites; she was the social, athletic girl, and I was the quiet, bookish one. But I had just shown her that I could throw a dart just as well as she could. For now, I was satisfied.

Chapter 10
Ameerah

I slapped my alarm clock to shut it off.

Across from my bed, I could see my calendar hanging on the wall. Today was Monday, June 10th. Something inside myself reminded me that I was dreading this day the night before, but for what reason, I couldn't recall.

I rolled out of bed and checked the time on my clock. It read 7:51 a.m. *Almost 8 o'clock*, I thought, rubbing the sleep out of my eyes. Cold gray light filtered through the shafts of my half-closed blinds, making a soft striped pattern on the floor. I opened my blinds all the way and peered outside. The rest of my neighborhood had been affected by the gray light. There was no sign of sun today.

Gloom and doom, I thought. After washing my face in the bathroom, I made my way down the staircase, my belly already growling for food. Usually on these types of days I was the first to awaken, so I was surprised to see Ali in the kitchen putting together a tomato-and-cheese sandwich. His hair damp from a shower and dressed in a solid colored button down, he looked up as I entered. "Good morning, princess," he greeted me.

"Hey," I replied, walking past him to open the fridge. "Why are you up so early?" I reached in and grabbed the milk carton, when suddenly, I realized. Today, June 10th, a Monday, was Ali's first day of work. "Oh," I said, before he could answer. "The job, huh?"

Ali glanced at me, then back at his sandwich. "That. Yeah."

Placing the milk on the counter, I watched Ali slide his sandwich into a plastic zipper bag, then put the zipper bag into a brown paper bag. He seemed to know I was watching him, but was avoiding my gaze.

"Coming back at 3, right?" I asked, even though I already knew the answer.

Ali nodded, closing up the paper bag.

"Can we shoot some hoops before you leave?" I asked. "Please?"

"Well... I leave in an hour," he said. "I've already showered, so I can't afford to get these clothes dirty. And I need to get Abdel-Hakeem to drive me to the place."

I frowned and looked back at the milk carton. "Your work is pretty important, huh," I said after a minute.

"Mmm," was all Ali said. I peeked at him through the corner of my eye. Just as I guessed. Phone again.

Important enough for you to ditch all our summer plans, I thought bitterly. Silently, I took the milk carton to the table. Today's breakfast was going to be the usual: corn flakes. And the cereal box was out of my reach, in the cabinet on top of the stove. "Ali?" I asked.

"Mmm?" he said again.

"Can you get the corn flakes for me, please?"

"Oh, sure." Still looking at his phone, Ali opened the cabinet and took out the cereal box. He then stood there in front of the stove, still texting away, with the cereal box in his hand.

"Umm, Ali," I said.

"Yeah?" He looked up from his phone at me, then at the cereal box in his hand. "Oh. Right. Sorry." Ali placed the box in front of me and then walked away, head bent to view his screen. I frowned. What was so important on his phone that he couldn't even pay attention to what he was doing? I watched him take his lunch bag off the counter and walk out of the kitchen.

I felt a twinge in my stomach. And it wasn't because I was hungry.

*   *   *

A soft breeze brushed the towering oak tree in our front yard. In the distance, chimes tinkled. The sky was still gray, and I couldn't see any sign of the sun coming to peek through. Our driveway was unusually empty. Abdel-Hakeem's car had left about an hour ago to take Ali to work.

It took me a while to realize that Ahmed was talking to me.

"Earth to Ameerah," said Ahmed. "Yo, you listening?"

"Uh-huh," I replied.

Ahmed sighed. "Dude, you've been sitting there forever. What are you looking at, anyway?"

I finally looked at him. "It's like I told you, Ahmed. I'm admiring the gloomy weather." In reality, I had been on the couch ever since I'd watched Ali leave for his work. His face as he waved goodbye to me was ingrained in my mind.

Ahmed didn't look convinced. "Well, whatever you're doing, you better wrap up soon because Abdel-Hakeem just called. He said he dropped Ali off and he's coming home to take us to the mall."

"The mall?" I asked, now turning my full attention to him. "What for?"

He shrugged. "Wedding stuff or something. So go take a

shower real quick before I do."

Considering Ahmed usually took at least fifteen minutes to shower, he was actually being nice right now. "Okay," I said, getting off the couch. Taking the stair steps two at a time, I reached my room and yanked my purple towel off its hook.

After my shower, I was back in the living room, dressed in a dark blue tee and black jeans. Just as I was pulling my hair back into a ponytail, Abdel-Hakeem pulled into the driveway. I hurried to open the door for him.

"Heeey, princess!" Abdel-Hakeem greeted me behind his black sunglasses. "Look who's all pretty and ready to go!"

Ready to go? I wasn't ready for anything today. I hadn't been ready for Ali to leave and forget I existed. "Yeah," I muttered stiffly. "Been ready for hours."

Abdel-Hakeem rambled on. "Would've come back way earlier. My bad, there was a traffic jam. Now where's Ahmed?"

"Showering. Why are you wearing sunglasses on a gloomy day?"

Abdel-Hakeem pushed his glasses up and rested them in his hair. "Gloomy day? Oh, right, I knew that. I just wanted to look cool. Uh, hey, did you say Ahmed was showering?"

I nodded.

"Ohhh no!" Abdel-Hakeem grasped his throat and pretended like he was suffocating. "Not showering! He takes *hours and hours* and..." Then he fell to his knees, feigning unconsciousness.

I finally managed to laugh a little. "Ahmed!" I shouted up the staircase. "Hurry up!"

"Why?" Ahmed's voice floated down the staircase. He

peeked down at us from the top of the stairs, a towel bound around his waist. "Why is Abdel-Hakeem on the floor?"

Abdel-Hakeem quickly hopped to his feet. "Because of you, bro! Get dressed and we're going!"

Chapter 11
Hanaan

"This one's just *be-yoo-tiful!*"

"Oh my god, the design? It's just exquisite!"

Rahima's and my mom's squeals and excited voices drifted through the screen door to the veranda where I was rocking on the porch swing. They had been looking at wedding dresses online for the past half hour and I was already beyond annoyed. Unable to handle it, I had stepped out to the veranda, attempting to drown out their voices by rocking as hard as I could on the squeaky swing.

Our visit during the weekend to the Sallehs' house had been disastrous, as far as I was concerned. According to my parents and Rahima, everything was already settled. After confirming that Rahima and The Guy, who I had started to name as such in my head, were ready to hitch up, everyone immediately started planning for the wedding. Rahima and The Guy began looking into apartments to rent and furniture to get for their new home and had hired a wedding planner to get all the event details ready before the date. They had decided that there was no reason to delay and wanted to have the wedding as soon as possible so they would have time to settle into their new home before Ramadan began. And because they both still had a bit of schoolwork to finish up, they were relying on the wedding planner to get the whole event organized and well-planned.

I had overheard enough over the past few days to figure out how all this had come about. Rahima and The Guy had met at school, but they hadn't seriously begun to get to know each other until this past year. And when they did get to know each other, they decided they wanted to spend the rest of their lives together. Ugh.

So my parents and Ameerah's parents had met up with each other, sometimes alone and sometimes with the potential bride and groom. For some reason, everyone seemed to love everyone else, and after talking it all over, the parents gave big thumbs ups and the marriage was officially on. I don't know where I was in all this. I later realized that all the meetings had probably happened when I was at Sr. Jamilah's house or at one of my clubs away from home. They hadn't included me in any of the discussions, hadn't asked to consider what I thought about all this. Because, of course, I had no say in the matter. No one cared what I thought, I told myself.

I was so busy rocking the swing harder and harder, feeling more hurt and furious by the minute, that I almost didn't notice an old car wheeze into our neighborhood and park in our driveway. I stopped rocking the swing when a young woman briskly stepped out of her car and headed towards me. The woman was of medium height, probably only a bit taller than me, but she carried herself confidently and gave a bit of a larger-than-life impression. She was dressed in a formal business suit and had her blonde hair tied back in a tight bun. It wasn't until she was nearly right in front of me that I noticed how young she actually was. She was probably younger than Rahima.

"Hey there," she greeted me once she reached the porch. "This is the Imraan residence, right?"

"Umm, yeah," I replied, a bit unsurely. "And you are...?"

"Kathy Kramer." She stretched out her hand to shake mine

and smiled at me. "I'd say you're the younger sister."

"Are you here to see Rahima, then?" I figured she must be the wedding planner, and it turned out I was right.

"Right you are. Could you let your sister know I'm here?"

I wasn't about to break my vow of never speaking to Rahima again, but I stepped into the house and called, "Mama, someone called Kathy Kramer is here and she wants to talk to your older daughter."

I heard Rahima exclaim, "She's here already?" Then there were footsteps rushing through the hall and suddenly she was standing in front of me.

"'Older daughter,' huh? That's what I am now?" She raised her eyebrows at me. I turned away, refusing to acknowledge her.

She sighed. "I wish you'd stop pretending I don't exist. But I guess I should be glad it means we don't have to argue anymore about who gets the last brownie." I knew she was smirking with her trademark twinkle in her eye, but I wasn't about to give in to her that easily. I focused on a loose thread hanging down from my t-shirt and twisted it around my finger.

Rahima wasted no more time trying to get me to talk to her. She opened the front door wide and greeted Kathy warmly. I only half listened as she asked Kathy to take her shoes off and offered to get some food for her before they began talking about wedding plans. While both of them were engrossed in chatter, I snuck a look at Rahima since I hadn't been this close to her in days. I was annoyed to see that her face was literally glowing, her eyes lighting up when she mentioned anything about the wedding.

And it hit me that Rahima was excited. She was excited to

get married, even though it meant leaving me, her only sister who she had claimed to love for so long. And on top of everything else I had been thinking about all morning, this thought hurt me the most.

I angrily strode through the hall towards the stairs, trying to escape all the wedding talk. Kathy's voice was loud and high-pitched as she confidently explained her plans. My mom and Rahima were chuckling at something she said. I stormed up the stairs two steps at a time and entered my room, feeling like a gray cloud. Without really thinking what I was doing, I snatched some paper from my desk and grabbed my trusty pen from my pencil holder. I yanked my window open and clumsily seated myself in Fajr's Shadow.

The fresh air and invigorating atmosphere of my special place usually calmed me down within moments when I was upset. But this time, my fury refused to relax as I scribbled down the words to a poem that was practically writing itself in my head. Half an hour later, as I accentuated my final line, I clutched the paper in my hand and held it up to read it to myself. But as I waved the paper in the air to smooth out the wrinkles, a sudden breeze blew in and caught the paper out of my hand. I desperately snatched into the air to retrieve it, but it flew beyond my grasp. *Oh my God, no! My poem!* Thinking fast, I hurriedly returned to my room and rushed down the stairs. I pulled open the front door and desperately looked around the front yard for my paper.

I wildly scanned the bushes and the expanse of grass before me but the paper was nowhere in sight. *Where is it?* I thought desperately and for a few moments my anger dissipated as I realized that the poem I had spent the past half hour on was gone. Giving up, I stormed back into the house and slammed the door behind me. My poem of betrayal had betrayed me. What irony.

Chapter 12
Ameerah

"So what exactly are we shopping for?" I asked, clicking on my seatbelt.

"Gonna do some ring shopping," Abdel-Hakeem replied.

I groaned. "Ring shopping? I thought we were going to do something fun! Why are you dragging us along?"

"Excuse me," Ahmed cut in. "*I'm* not being dragged."

"Are you saying you *want* to do ring shopping?" I asked Ahmed incredulously.

"Uhh, no! I'm going to Gaming Life to check out the latest video games."

"Come on, Ameerah, don't you want to help your poor brother out?" Abdel-Hakeem said, adjusting his rearview mirror. "Mama was supposed to come and help me out, but she was called into work. You can't expect me to pick out the perfect ring by myself, can you?"

"But I hate jewelry shopping," I protested.

"Not as much as jewelry hates you," Ahmed smirked at me.

I stuck out my tongue at him, even though his words rang true in my mind. When I had gone to get my ears pierced, I squealed and squirmed so much that the staple gun almost impaled my nostrils. In the end, everyone decided to just give up, and my mom bought clip-ons for me instead. Aside from that, the most I wore was a bracelet. Jewelry just wasn't my thing.

"Alrighty! Let's go!" my eldest brother said, slapping a hand on the wheel. "Oh — does everyone have their seatbelt on?"

With a sigh, I pouted and gazed out the window. *Let's just get this over with.*

"I've had it on for hours," Ahmed exaggerated. "Let's just get going and hurry up."

"Why don't you hurry up and get your license?" Abdel-Hakeem joked. "Wait up. Everyone say your duas[14] before I head off."

I began to quietly recite the travel dua to myself, when Abdel-Hakeem interrupted, "Eh, where y'all's voices at? Louder so I can hear 'em, please!"

Ahmed and I sighed, and we recited along with our brother:

"Allahu akbar, Allahu akbar, Allahu akbar. Subhaanalladhee sakharalanaa haadha wa maa kunna lahuu muqrineen, wa innaa ila rabbinaa la munqaliboon."

"Awesome," said Abdel-Hakeem. He pressed his foot on the gas, and we were off.

Throughout the ride, I envisioned all the types of rings we might have to look at. *This better not take too long*, I thought wistfully. *After all, it is just a ring!*

Finally, we pulled into the giant parking lot of the Bon Monde Mall.

"Alright, I'm out," Ahmed announced as soon as the car stopped.

---

[14]Supplications

[15]Travel supplication: Allah is the Most Great. Allah is the Most Great. Allah is the Most Great. Glory is to Him Who has provided this for us though we could never have had it by our efforts. Surely, unto our Lord we are returning.

"You got your phone on you?" Abdel-Hakeem asked as he turned off the engine.

"Yeah," said Ahmed.

"Alright then. You go to your store while I take Princess to look at rings. Get out of the car, y'all!"

Once inside the mall, Ahmed hurried away to Gaming Life, and I grudgingly walked behind Abdel-Hakeem into Hemsworth Jewelers. The air conditioning planted goosebumps on my arms, and the cold yellow light from above reflected off of all the jewelry in the store. Crystal, gold and silver surrounded me from all sides until I began to feel dizzy. "What are we supposed to do now?" I asked my brother helplessly.

Abdel-Hakeem grinned at me and led me over to a tiered glass table in the middle of the room. Dozens of shining rings sparkled through the glass, and I watched Abdel-Hakeem gaze at them with wide, eager eyes.

"Help me find the most perfect ring for Rahima, okay?"

"They all look the same to me," I replied.

Abdel-Hakeem shook his head at me and then reached into his back pocket for something. I gaped at him when he unfolded a paper packet that had the words "A Guide to Choosing the Perfect Ring" written in bold on top. I groaned and slumped my shoulders, leaning on the table for support. *Is he serious?!*

My brother spread out the papers in front of him and began to carefully compare the rings behind the glass with the descriptions on paper, mumbling all the while.

Soon enough a friendly-faced woman appeared behind the glass table and greeted us in a cheerful voice, probably summoned by the sound of Abdel-Hakeem talking to himself. "How can I help you today?" She nodded at the papers Abdel-Hakeem had spread out and grinned. "Someone's gonna be a lucky girl, huh?"

"If I can ever find the right ring!" Abdel-Hakeem responded.

His mutterings were beginning to get on my nerves as he contemplated all sorts of things I had never even thought about in my life. Would Rahima like one with a giant gemstone on it? Or a pearl? What about the tiny three-studded kind? What if she doesn't want gems on her ring? Maybe she would want the giant kind of ring that covers half of your finger. Ugh, so many decisions!

"It. Is. Just. A. Ring," I said, trying to get his attention. "A round object you put around your finger."

The lady noticed me then and emitted a hearty laugh.

"Don't worry, young lady. It will be your day soon enough."

What?! As I tried to wrap my head around this comment, the lady turned her attention back to my brother and offered to bring out some rings from the display. I only half listened as Abdel-Hakeem repeated his specifications to her.

Something simple, yet stylish. Something with unique, but with recognizable elements. Something that stands out, but isn't bulky or overweight.

"This pearl-studded silver ring may be just what you need." The jewelry lady was holding up a ring while Abdel-Hakeem peered closely at it. I took a glance at it and had to admit that, for a ring, it looked pretty attractive, but my brother was frowning a bit.

"Hmm… can I see that in gold, if you don't mind?"

"Sure!" The lady carefully lay the ring down and leaned over to bring out another set of rings. "Now this one is studded with tiny diamonds as opposed to this other one that is simply one large diamond. And…" She made a big show of pulling out another ring from under the table. "This one has encrusted pearls embedded between the diamonds."

Abdel-Hakeem took a long, hard look at the choices in front of him, turning from one to the other again and again, his brow creased in thought.

"She's gonna marry you no matter what ring you get her, bro," I groaned as he made a motion to ask to see another set of rings.

"You're not much help, Ameerah," Abdel-Hakeem teased, shaking his finger at me.

His teasing made me break out into a grudging smile, even though I wasn't exactly feeling happy. "Abdel-Hakeeeeem! This is taking forever. Are you sure you can't just pick one and go?"

"I can't just get any old ring, Ameerah."

"Okay, fine. I'll just sit over there until you're done." And I walked away towards a small bench situated at the back of the shop beside a rack of bracelets.

*   *   *

After what seemed like hours later, Abdel-Hakeem finally picked out his idea of the 'perfect ring' for his beloved Rahima and paid for it at the cash register. We picked up Ahmed from the game store and headed home.

The car clock read 12:34 p.m. *Ali's going to be home in less than three hours,* I thought. I was starting to feel a bit cheerful since that awful shopping expedition was finally over and began singing along with Ahmed to Abdel-Hakeem's nasheed playlist. Currently playing was *Number One For Me* by Maher Zain.

The song suddenly stopped abruptly. Abdel-Hakeem had paused it.

"Hey!" Ahmed and I protested. "We weren't done!"

Abdel-Hakeem chuckled. "Tell me, who's up for some ice cream?"

"Ohhh! Me! Me!"

"Thought so!" Abdel-Hakeem turned the wheel to the right, arriving at my go-to ice cream joint: Polar Point. "We have arrived," my eldest brother announced dramatically, as if he were a flight attendant. "Please remove your seatbelts and exit the car safely. No arguing or slamming the door is permitted. Thank you."

I laughed and did exactly as I was told, then followed my brothers inside the shop. Ahmed went ahead to order his usual: a cookies-and-cream and cookie dough double-dipper, topped with chocolate syrup.

"So what'll it be today, chocolate or mint chip?" Abdel-Hakeem asked me.

I crossed my arms over my chest. "Abdel-Hakeem! You know what I like!"

He chuckled. "Right, right. Strawberry cheesecake and orange sorbet, right?"

"Right!"

Abdel-Hakeem ordered mine and bought a chocolate cone for himself. When our cones were ready, we ate outside at our favorite table: the one closest to the edge with the blue and yellow umbrella. I squinted out at the cars running down the streets. For now, the sun was peeking through the clouds, but rain didn't look far away.

Abdel-Hakeem cleared his throat loudly. "May I have your attention, people! We are gathered here today due to the patience shown by our princess Ameerah during the ring shopping trip. As much as it was tedious for me, it was for her, so I have decided to reward her with an outing to her favorite ice cream joint." He held out his cone to me as if it were a microphone. "What say you, Ameerah Salleh?"

"Well, I have to say, that was the worst shopping trip I ever experienced," I said. "But I'm so glad it's over now." I took a huge bite out of my ice cream.

Ahmed shook his head at me. "You're basically the only person I know who bites her ice cream," he commented. "Weirdo."

I took a bigger bite just to annoy him.

"And just how many people do you know?" Abdel-Hakeem joked. "Judging by all that time you spend in your room..."

Ahmed grunted. "Aw, shut up."

When we'd finished our cones, we headed back home. By now it was 1:22 p.m., and Ahmed and I were again listening to nasheeds. Our open windows and Abdel-Hakeem's fast driving was letting in a lovely breeze, lifting our spirits for every second of the drive.

The moment we walked towards our front door, thunder rolled overhead, and rain pattered down, slowly intensifying. Thankfully, we had reached our door by then, and we were under the safety of our roof. Nevertheless, I pushed Abdel-Hakeem to hurry with the keys.

"Hurry, we're gonna be soaked!" I said. "God, if I'd known

it was going to rain today, I'd have brought an umbrella!" It seemed that, despite all the preparation Abdel-Hakeem had done for the ring shopping, he had not checked the weather forecast before leaving the house.

Abdel-Hakeem quickly unlocked the door, and we all stumbled inside, kicking off our sneakers and leaving them in a messy pile beside the door. It was funny seeing our shoes in a jumble like that; typically, if Ali had been present, he would have lectured us about keeping the shoes paired up neatly beside the door, and if our shoes were muddy or wet, we would have to leave them outside until they dried.

Ali was always on our backs to make sure we kept everything clean. It was ridiculous how tidy his room was. Ali actually shared a room with Ahmed, but his side was so much significantly cleaner than Ahmed's that it looked like a whole other room. And Ahmed was the messiest person I knew. Worse than me.

The rest of us had grown so accustomed to Ali's tidying rules that Abdel-Hakeem now remarked, "Looks like we have it easy today, eh, guys?"

Ahmed laughed. "Totally. No Neat Freak Ali here to bother us today!"

No Neat Freak Ali here, I repeated in my mind. I had to admit, his cleanliness did annoy me sometimes, but today I missed it. I missed him. Already.

Thunder rumbled outside and rain fell in sheets. I'd always disliked rain. It was the culprit behind postponed soccer games, canceled playdates, and sleepless nights. It was what darkened the house and set a depressing mood. And usually on rainy days, everyone stuck themselves in their rooms, honing their hobbies or just relaxing. I didn't like those kinds of days. I wanted everyone to be together in the same room, spending time with each other.

Another wave of thunder rolled outside, causing me to shudder. Allahhumma sayyiban naafi'ah[16], I recited to myself.

Abdel-Hakeem and Ahmed left their shoes in a mess beside the door and hurried upstairs to their rooms; Ahmed to try out his new video game, and Abdel-Hakeem to probably nap. What was I left to do if I couldn't go out and shoot hoops? If Ali hadn't gotten that job, he and I would be playing board games or telling scary stories in a homemade fort. If Ali hadn't gotten that job, he'd get me to watch some of his animations and voice some of his characters.

If Ali hadn't gotten that job... everything would be perfect, I thought as I paired up everyone's shoes neatly beside the door.

---

[16]Rain supplication: Oh Allah, make this beneficial rain.

Chapter 13
Hanaan

As if to make up for keeping the wedding a secret from me for so long, my mom kept telling me every single detail about the event that I had no interest in knowing. My mind was bursting with the description of every single bit of sequins on Rahima's outfit, the arrangement of tables and chairs in the wedding hall, the names of family we barely knew who were coming for the reception. All the information about the wedding was making it all seem so real, and I didn't want it to be real. I wanted it all to just be a nightmare, one I would wake up from and think about for a bit, but then laugh off and get on with life.

Rahima was driving me nuts, as well. As much as I tried to avoid her, she still seemed to be everywhere. She'd accepted that I didn't want to talk to her and began directing long speeches at me without expecting any response.

"I declare! This eggplant is the tastiest thing I've ever eaten," she exclaimed one particularly quiet afternoon at the dining table. "It's like squishy, but not too squishy, and you can see the little specks, but oh my dear goodness, it's such a pleasurable meal and just think how my twenty-two years of life have led to this moment of eggplant enjoyment."

Normally, I would've interrupted Rahima right away saying, "Eww, no, stop!" but my vow of silence stood as a barrier. My dad was out at a meeting for work and my mom was taking a shower. Rahima and I were alone at the table, and all I could do was listen as she continued her rambling.

"Most of my friends hate eggplant, and I guess I can understand that the texture might be a little off-putting, especially when it's all mixed up together like this, but the taste, though! I cannot even begin to explain."

I don't care! I screamed in my head, but she just wouldn't stop.

"I like eggplant cooked in all sorts of ways: baked, fried, grilled. You know, I just realized that I have never tasted eggplant in my life that I haven't liked. I literally like every kind of eggplant ever. Except…well, I've never eaten it raw, but that is another thing entirely. Who would eat eggplant raw?"

The thing about sisters who are as close as Rahima and I are to each other is that we know exactly how to get on each other's nerves. But Rahima wasn't done yet.

"Oh my, you know what I just realized? I've never talked to Abdel-Hakeem about eggplant. I don't even know if he likes eggplant. Goodness, what do we even talk about if we haven't talked about eggplant? I mean something as important as this and we haven't even discussed it!"

Okay, now this was getting ridiculous. I didn't even care that she was talking about The Guy. I just wanted her to stop talking about eggplant.

"Is eggplant the only vegetable that is purple on the outside? Oh wait, what about turnips? Are turnips even purple? Oh, purply, purply purple."

That did it. My fork clattered onto my plate as I dropped it out of frustration.

"Maaamaaa! Where are you? Your daughter is weirding me

out and I can't stand it!"

Rahima smirked at me. "Knew it wouldn't take much to get a reaction out of you."

"Wouldn't take much?" I muttered to myself incredulously as my mom entered the dining room, her hair wrapped up in a peach-colored towel.

"Hey, hey, what's all the fuss?" she asked breezily.

"Your daughter is driving me nuts," I hissed.

"My poor daughter. Leave her alone, Rahima. Let the girl eat in peace."

"So she can enjoy the eggplant, huh?" Rahima snorted.

"She's crazy," I muttered, jamming a forkful of the eggplant into my mouth.

"What's that, Hanaan? You have something to say to me?" Rahima lay her fork down and looked right at me, raising her eyebrows in a quirky way.

I avoided her gaze and turned to face my mom so it couldn't be supposed that I was talking to my sister. "She just wants attention, and I am not gonna give it to her. Just because everyone else is adoring her doesn't mean she can get adoration from me, too."

"Hanaan," my mom said gently. "She's still your older sister."

I bit my tongue when the words, "I don't care" popped up into my head. "If she wants attention, she can get it from the very lovely Sallehs. I'm sure Ameerah Salleh will be a much better sister than I ever was." I gulped up the last of my food and stood up to toss my plate in the sink.

"Hanaan Amina Imraan!" Rahima was no longer joking around. "What are you saying? How could you think...how could you even suppose that anyone could replace you?"

I felt a sharp pang hearing Rahima say my full name, re-membering that she was the one who had named me, once upon a time. *It's not that hard, Rahima, and you'd realize that if you sat and thought about it for a second.* Aloud I said, "It's getting late, and Sr. Jamilah is expecting me."

My mom sighed, but she nodded. "You don't want to keep her waiting."

I heard Rahima let out an exasperated sigh as I hastily washed my hands and reached for my bag that was on the count-er. "Hanaan, you can't just block me out forever. We need to talk about this."

Ignoring her, I hoisted my bag over my shoulder and head-ed to the front door. "Assalamu alaikum, Mama," I said deliberate-ly and left the house.

As soon as Sr. Jamilah opened the door to her apartment, I could tell that something was different. She greeted me as warmly as ever and still had that infectious smile, but she was eyeing me in a strange way. I could sense that there was something on the tip of her tongue, and I desperately tried to sidetrack her with a bunch of random remarks.

"Hamza's outfit is so cute. I don't think I've seen it before."

Sr. Jamilah raised her eyebrow. "It's just a t-shirt and shorts."

"Yeah, but, like, the stripes? They suit him so well."

"Well, he seems to like it."

I glanced around desperately for something else to comment on. "Hey! You changed the batteries of that old clock."

"Yup, I did it this morning. I finally decided I had enough of the wrong time on the wall every day."

"Yeah, the right time is good to have…so, you know, you know what the right time is…" Awkwardly, I shifted my bag on my shoulder. "…and not the wrong time."

Sr. Jamilah gave me an extra long look before saying,

"Yeah, I guess you're right."

"I finished all the books you gave me to read for history last time," I said quickly. "They were pretty good."

"Glad you liked them." Sr. Jamilah sat Hamza down a bit away from us and placed a few toys next to him. This was usually our cue to get to our studies while Hamza was occupied, but Sr. Jamilah didn't get out any of her books. She sat down across from me on the sofa and gave me a grin. It was a half grin, the kind that is meant to lighten a serious conversation.

"I hear you've been hating on Rahima, huh?"

There. She said it. Her words hung in the air for a few moments.

"What's she been telling you?" I asked defensively, at that moment remembering that Sr. Jamilah was basically best friends with my sister.

"Dude, relax. Rahima's just concerned about you."

"That's good to know." I kind of regretted saying that the next moment because it sounded rude, but Sr. Jamilah didn't seem to notice.

"I know it's all kind of my fault so I wish you'd blame me

instead of her."

At this, I was confused. What did Sr. Jamilah have to do with any of this?

"I was the one who broke the news to you. I know that couldn't have been nice for you, and I wish I had thought before saying anything."

"Yeah? But that doesn't change the fact that Rahima kept it a secret from me for so long."

"Well, did you ask her why she didn't tell you in the beginning?"

"She just has a bunch of lame excuses."

Sr. Jamilah was quiet for a moment as she carefully weighed her words. "This is going to be a big change for both of you, and weddings can be a pretty stressful time. I remember during my wedding when everything kept going wrong on the morning of the event. One of our big problems was that my brother was supposed to go to the flower shop, Botanica Flowers, a few hours before the reception. But it turned out that Botanica is never open on Fridays and my wedding was on a Friday evening. We were all in a panic, but alhamdulillah, it all turned out well in the end. We got the flowers from Her Majesty instead, but they were so much more expensive. And you know what else happened that day?"

I cleared my throat a little too loudly and Sr. Jamilah hastily returned to her topic. "So, yeah, my point is it probably won't help if you keep avoiding your sister."

"I know you want to help," I said slowly but firmly. "But I think Rahima should be the one to dig herself out of her own hole."

Sr. Jamilah chuckled. "She told me you're stubborn, so I can't say I haven't been warned."

I didn't want to hear anymore about the conversation between my sister and my tutor, so I reached into my bag and pulled out my books. "So…school time?" I said.

"Okay then, Queen of Changing the Subject." And she pulled the table closer to us as I opened up my textbook.

Chapter 14
Ameerah

Tap-taptaptap, I rapped on Ali's door.

"Who is it?" Ahmed called.

"Your sister!" I called back.

"Which one?"

I laughed. "Uh, the only one!"

"Well, what does the only sister want?"

"I wanna talk to Ali! We're supposed to do our weekend exercises!"

"'Kay," Ahmed replied. "Wait."

A few seconds later, Ali opened the door. He brushed his rumpled bangs away from his face and squinted at me through sleepy eyes. "Morning, Ameerah," he mumbled. "What's up?"

"What's up?" I asked. "I'm up!" I gestured to the outfit I was wearing; a neon blue sports tank and black sweats with white stripes down the sides. My hair was pulled back into a high pony-tail, and I'd added a headband to catch droplets of sweat. "C'mon, Ali, our weekend exercises!" I said. "Ring a bell?"

"Oh, yeah." Ali yawned, stretching his huge, muscular arms into the air. He then stood there for a moment, just trying to keep his eyes open, and finally he looked at me. "I really don't want to mess up our routine, Ameerah, but I don't think I can exercise right now. I stayed up really late last night working on something and I need to catch up on sleep." At the sight of my crestfallen expression, Ali quickly added, "You can go ahead by yourself, can't you?"

He gave a lopsided smile.

My face in a pout, I shrugged. "Yeah, I guess."

"There, that's a good princess." Ali patted my shoulder. "Go on now."

I began to walk away, head hanging, and as I looked back, Ali was closing his door.

"He didn't even say sorry," I muttered, pouting harder. I began to walk down the staircase. "Fine. I'll do it alone."

Throughout the week, I had attempted several times to get Ali's attention, but his response was always something like, "Not now, Ameerah," or "You can go ahead without me." So eventually, I did end up doing things without him. I continued our green smoothie diet, jogged around the neighborhood before Maghrib[17] time, rollerbladed to the park, and watched a documentary on how certain foods were processed in factories.

Once downstairs, I pulled on my black and white sneakers. "I'll be out in the driveway!" I shouted to whoever was listening, then opened the front door. The sun had finally decided to peek between the clouds, and for now, the rainfall had ceased. On my way to our driveway, I basked in the faint sunlight. The temperature was perfectly warm, with a cool breeze swirling by every now and then.

I started off with the usuals: twenty-five jumping jacks, a few stretches, sit-ups, and push-ups. Then I moved on to squats. Squats were the most difficult part of my workout and I always left them for last. Ali did them with weights, something I couldn't yet do, but strived for.

---

[17]Sunset prayer

I put my arms straight out in front of me with my back straight and feet evenly spaced apart. Then I leaned forward a little and bent my knees, and I maintained this position for ten seconds. "One...two...three..." I grunted. Already, my headband was dripping with sweat and my thighs felt like they were on fire. When ten seconds were up, I straightened up again, then repeated the exercise. I could feel my face reddening, and I squeezed my eyes shut in pain. My heart pounded so hard it nearly blocked out the sounds of cars rushing by. "One...two...three...four..."

And then I couldn't hold it anymore. On the fifth second, I let a huge breath escape me as I stood up straight. The fire bolted from my thighs and circulated around my body.

"I can't... do this anymore," I panted as I dragged myself back to the front door. My head was buzzing and I was in dire need of a drink. *I usually shoot for ten. Why can't I do ten today?*

I kicked off my sneakers and left them outside the house, still lost in my muddle about my failure to finish squatting. Something was missing. And as I spotted a pair of size 11 sandals primly placed beside each other on the doormat, I knew what today's session had lacked.

I know I could have gone on if Ali was with me, I thought. It was true. Typically, he would squat alongside me, encouraging me to push harder, saying that I could do it. His words never failed to help me, and I always reached ten. Today would have been no different if only he had been present.

I made a beeline for the kitchen, grabbing my favorite glass and pressing it to the water dispenser in our fridge. The glass hadn't even reached the halfway mark before I snatched it away from the dispenser, chugging up that water like my life depended on it. The water calmed my heartbeat, and my body began to cool down.

Alright, shower time. I hurried upstairs to my room and yanked off my headband, my socks, and my hair tie. I unhooked my purple towel from the hook on my door, and was on my way to the bathroom before my mother stopped me.

"Oh, Ameerah, you're about to take a shower? Good. We're about to go shopping because you guys need new clothes before Abdel-Hakeem's wedding."

I opened my mouth to reply, but my mom finished with, "We're leaving in ten minutes," then headed for her room.

New clothes, I thought as I closed the bathroom door behind me. *Ugh, does that mean I have to wear a dress?* I owned very few dresses, and the ones I did own reached just below my knees. I hated the feeling of cloth swishing around my feet. It made me feel trapped, with no freedom to run around, and I was always having to worry about tripping. The fanciest I could ever dress myself was a short dress and ankle boots. I couldn't do hair very well, so my mom was usually the one who put it in braids, buns, and updos. But I'd never been to a wedding before. What if my mom was going to make me dress even more extravagantly for the wedding?

Baba drove the van to the Bon Monde Mall. He was talking with Mama and Abdel-Hakeem about wedding plans, which I didn't care to hear about. The only thing I'd caught, and what caused me to zone out from the conversation in the first place, was that we were going to Hanaan's house for dinner after Maghrib.

Since then, I'd crossed my arms, huffily blew a stray hair

away from my face, and began to mentally prepare myself for yet another awkward encounter with Rahima's younger sister. Sure, the girl was alright. I mean, she threw darts with me. I hadn't expected someone like her to make a bull's eye after two tries only. But she was homeschooled, which made my mother think it was all the more appropriate to impose the same torture on me, as well.

Grr.

Beside me, Ahmed nodded his head in rhythm to his tunes. I didn't know whether or not he knew that I could hear Harris J's Salam Alaikum practically blasting out of his earphones, but I tried ignoring it.

Ali sat in front of me, and my parents had made him leave his phone at home, which made me happy. Now he had no choice but to talk to me. I tapped him on the shoulder. "Ali. Yo."

He turned to face me. "Mmm. Yes, Ameerah?"

I grinned. "Today I made the smoothie out of broccoli, celery, strawberries, and lemonade. With an addition of chia seeds and oatmeal."

About a year ago, Ali and I decided we would go a green smoothie diet to improve our physical health. The year before, we'd tried a juicing diet, and our health improved so drastically that we decided to take it a step further. Every Saturday, we would blend a combination of a variation of fruits and veggies, along with a fluid like water, milk, or juice. The smoothies didn't taste particularly delicious, but Ali and I didn't mind. We were always so excited to see how our bodies changed every week. Abdel-Hakeem and Ahmed always shook their heads at us, saying they would never be able to eat their fruits and veggies together. "And especially not in smoothie form. Yuck!" Ahmed would say.

Ali smiled. "Sounds good," he said. "How was it?"

"It was alright," I said. With a knowing glint in my eye, I added, "Wish you could have had some."

"Yeah, well..." Ali looked away for a bit, then at me again. "How was the workout?"

The workout. "Well... it went well until I got to the squats," I admitted. "I only went as far as two, and on the second one I could only count five seconds."

"Five seconds?" Ali raised his thick eyebrows. "You usually go for ten though. What went wrong?"

I squinted at him. Didn't he know he was the one who could help me get to ten? *And what went wrong?* He knew what went wrong. His lack of presence! But I didn't want to rant to him in front of everybody, so I just said, "Oh, the weather, I guess."

"Mmm." Ali nodded slowly.

"Kids, I want all of us to have a family theme color on the wedding day," Mama announced.

Ahmed grunted and yanked out his earbuds. "What?"

"Anything but green!" I piped up. "And I'm not going to wear a dress to the wedding!"

My parents laughed. "Of course you're wearing a dress to the wedding," Mama said. "How about we dress in red?"

"I look like a jerk in red," Ahmed muttered.

"You look like a jerk in everything," Abdel-Hakeem said.

"If I have to wear a dress," I continued, "it has to match my criteria." I counted off my fingers. "It can't be any longer than below my knees, can't have sequins, can't be made of itchy fabric, and it *must* be either *blue* or *purple*."

Mama sighed. "Okay then. Blue or purple?"

"Doesn't really matter," said Abdel-Hakeem with a shrug.

"Purple, I guess," said Ali.

"They're the same thing!" said Ahmed.

Mama shot an expectant look at Baba.

"Oh, uh, blue," he said absentmindedly, turning the van into the Bon Monde parking lot.

"Well," said Mama, "that wasn't very helpful. How about this. You men dress in blue, and the ladies dress in purple? How does that sound, hmm?"

"Sure," said Baba.

Abdel-Hakeem shrugged.

"I guess," said Ali.

"Is there a difference?" Ahmed asked.

"That sounds good," I said, satisfied.

"Alhamdulillah," my mother sighed dramatically.

We pulled into a parking space, and Baba turned off the van. "Come," he said, opening his door.

Ahmed grunted again and stuck his earbuds back in.

Once inside the mall, I tapped my mother on the arm.

"Hey, Mama, do I really need to wear a dress?" I asked.

Mama smiled. "Of course you do, princess! It's your brother's wedding. You have to look nice."

I frowned. "But Mama, jeans look nice, too! Or even sweats. What's wrong with those?"

"Those are informal pieces of clothing," said my mother. "Come now, Ameerah, don't be silly. You look adorable in dresses."

But I don't want to look adorable! I huffed and followed her inside the store. While my father and the boys headed for the suits and dress shirts, my mother took me to the dresses rack. These dresses looked like they had been thrown into an ocean; they hung in a blinding array of blues, greens, and purples. I flipped through each of them with haste, hoping to find at least something I liked, just to get this whole dress dilemma over with. Finally, what caught my eye was a vibrant, dark purple dress, made of soft, silky fabric. Silver jewels ran around the neckline all the way to the waist in a beautiful pattern. The sleeves just barely covered my shoulders, and the flowy skirt reached a few inches past my knees.

"Aw, sweet!" I squealed, snatching the dress off the rack. "Mama, this one is cool!"

My mother had gone to the other side of the rack, and looked at me when I called her. She walked around the rack to analyze the dress I'd picked. "Hmm, this is nice," she said, then took it out of my hand. "Hmm. Very nice, in fact."

"So can I have it, Mama?" I asked, disregarding her 'hmm'-ing. "It's gotta be that or jeans."

At that, my mother took her eyes off the dress to look at me. "In that case, you may." She smiled and lay the dress back in my hands. "It is very cute."

Cute? Eww! Why would anyone call a piece of clothing *cute?* Why did my mom use that word so much? Wrinkling my nose, I hung the dress by its hanger on my arm.

"Now, let's get you some matching shoes and jewelry," said my mother, leading me to the shoe area.

"Jewelry?" I exclaimed. "But I—"

"I know, I know," Mama cut in. "You're terrible at wearing jewelry. But this time I really want you to wear jewelry to the wedding and you can't lose it. Okay?"

"Okay, Mama."

I didn't mind shoe shopping all that much. I loved the fresh, leathery smell of the shoe area. The only thing that exasperated me was having to put on and take off a bunch of different sized shoes.

Let's see, I thought, counting off my fingers again. *If I have to get new shoes, they can't be sandals or sneakers or flip-flops, because I have those already. And I don't like high heels. If I'm getting new shoes, they have to be ankle boots. Specifically ankle boots, and nothing else.*

"So, Ameerah, what kind of shoes do you want?" my mother asked. With a smirk, she added, "Other than sneakers and cleats?"

I told her my list of shoe criteria, to which she 'hmm'-ed again. Then she led me to the boots, where she told me to "feel free." I grunted at that, because for the past week I had not felt very free at all. But I walked into the aisle, looking up and down for the perfect boots.

For the longest time, I couldn't find what I was looking for, and my mom even said, "Maybe you can try out high heels," to which I immediately protested. I liked shoes with elevation, but no higher than one inch.

Finally, I found what I wanted: open-toe suede ankle boots with a slightly raised heel. Just what I was looking for! I hastened to find my size, then grabbed the box and thrust it in my mother's face. "Found them, Mama!"

"Hmm," Mama said immediately.

I knew she was trying to make me laugh, but she only annoyed me more than I already was about so many things that were happening. "Mamaaa!" I whined.

"Fine, don't laugh," my mother said. She opened the box and studied the shoes, after which she put them back in the box. "These are pretty. Don't you want to try them on first, though?"

"They probably fit anyway, Mama! I'm size 5, they're size 5. Do I have to?"

"Yes, you do, dear. Sometimes the type of shoe affects the way it fits. Now, come on, sit down, and try them on." She handed the box to me.

"Okay, but I'm only trying on one shoe," I said, picking out the right-foot boot. I kicked off my right sandal and slid my foot into the boot. It was a bit of a loose fit, but they were comfortable.

"How are they?" asked Mama.

"Kinda loose, but they're okay," I said hastily, mostly because I wanted to get this thing over with. I pulled off the boot, placed it back in the box, and slipped into my sandal.

"You'll grow into them." Mama closed the box. "Alright, perfect. We're done here."

"Thank God!" I said, throwing my hands into the air. "Now can we buy the jewelry that I'm not going to wear and get out of here so I can enjoy the few hours left of this day before we go to Hanaan's house?" I crossed my arms at my mother.

Mama sighed. "Ameerah, don't you like Hanaan? She's a very nice and sweet girl. Didn't you guys have fun when she came over?"

I shrugged. "As much fun as hearing about a postponed

soccer game, sure."

My mother said no more, and brought me to the jewelry area. It was lit very brightly by several lights in various areas I couldn't locate, and it reflected off of all the rings, earrings, bracelets, and necklaces enclosed in a glass case. All the glitter and shiny stuff was beginning to give me a minor migraine. It was taking me back to the ring expedition with Abdel-Hakeem.

I followed Mama to the clip-on earring rack. "Alright, Ameerah," my mother said, turning to me with her arms crossed. "Can you promise me you won't make this difficult?"

I widened my eyes. "*Difficult,* Mama? I haven't been difficult at all!"

Upon hearing that, my mother's mouth twitched, but she cleared her throat quickly and waved her hand at me. "Sure. Whatever you say. Go ahead and find your earrings."

I finally presented a pair of climber earrings to Mama. Then we met Baba and the boys at the cash register. I bounced on my toes, anxious to finally finish the shopping trip. Abdel-Hakeem was grinning widely. "Oh my God, you guys are going to look so *good* at my wedding!" he almost squealed.

"Pfft," Ahmed huffed. "I look good all the time."

I pursed my lips. "What a lie."

"You said earlier that you look like a jerk in red!" Abdel-Hakeem laughed.

"Well, that's different," Ahmed said, holding up one hand. "Red is an awful color. It's like blood, and blood is disgusting."

"You're disgusting," Abdel-Hakeem returned.

I looked up at Ali, expecting him to defend his favorite

color, but he made no comment. He seemed lost in his thoughts, which made me curious, because he was usually on top of everything and knew what he was doing.

"Hey, what are y'all wearing?" I asked, standing on my tiptoes to try and see the transaction over the counter.

"Clothes," Ahmed replied.

I stuck my tongue between my brace-bound teeth at him.

"Ha," I said. "I meant to the wedding."

"Still clothes, hopefully," said Ahmed.

I rolled my eyes.

Once we were finally home, Mama detagged all of our new clothes and arranged them neatly in our coat closet. I brought my new shoes and earrings to my room, placing the shoes in my closet, and the earrings in my fairly empty "jewelry box" which was really just an old perfume box.

Since there were several hours until we had to go to Hanaan's house, I decided I'd go and watch another documentary. *Ali better be up for it*, I thought as I determinedly walked to his room. *It isn't humanly possible to be so busy without rest for all seven days of the week.* I knocked on my brother's door, and after a few seconds, Ahmed quietly opened the door. "Yo, what do you want?" he asked in a hushed whisper. "If it's Ali, forget it. He's trying to nap."

"Oh." I studied a deep crease in the floor. "Well, okay. I'll forget it." I met his gaze again. "Thanks though."

I guess he does take his rest from work sometimes. Just not the way I like it.

Chapter 15
Hanaan

"Rahima! Where is the fancy tablecloth? It's not in the cupboard."

"I noticed a stain on it and tried to clean it so it's still drying in the bathroom."

"What? Will it be dry enough on time?"

"I don't know, but where's Baba? The front step has a loose nail sticking out, and I can't find the tool box!"

"He went to the store to pick up some drinks and…what is that smell? Is something…"

"The lasagna!"

I entered the kitchen just in time to see Rahima dash in with a panicked expression on her face. She peered into the oven and breathed a sigh of relief. "It's all good!" she called to my mom. "Didn't burn yet."

I shook my head as I poured myself a glass of water and wiped a few strands of hair from my sweaty face. The whole house was in a flurry of anticipation because the Sallehs were coming for dinner. With the way everyone was intent on making everything spotlessly clean and perfect, it was like we were hosting royalty.

I watched Rahima as she put on two oven mitts and carefully took out the large sizzling tray of lasagna. She turned off the oven and took a few moments to breathe in the delightful aroma of all the delicious food cooking.

I walked past her to put my glass in the sink, but she didn't seem to notice me. I dropped my glass a little noisily and waited for her to react, but her eyes were still concentrated on the food. I began to feel offended. *Is she ignoring me?*

Just then, the doorbell rang. That Rahima did notice. Her head flew up and she looked wildly in the direction of the front door. "Mama, what time is it? They can't be here now, can they? I'm not ready at all!" She was wearing a worn t-shirt and a pair of pants covered in dust, and her hair was a mess. I could feel the panic rising in my normally cool and collected sister, and it was strange to see her this way.

"Assalamu alaikum!" My dad greeted us loudly as he announced his entrance.

"Oh, phew! It's just Baba." Rahima relaxed a bit.

"Yup, it's just me," my dad joked, entering the kitchen with a few grocery bags in his hands.

"Baba!" Rahima exclaimed. "The front step. It's -"

"Loose, I know," he replied, patting her reassuringly on the shoulder. "Don't worry about it. I'm going to fix it right now."

"You're the best! Now I just have to double-check that the living room is fine before I can change." And the two left the kitchen, neither of them acknowledging my presence.

An hour later, the fancy tablecloth was laid out on the dining table, all the food impressively spread out on top. Every bit of the house was shining and spotlessly clean. Both of my parents were wearing crisp, formal outfits, and my mom had insisted that I wear a fancy outfit, too. Rahima was still in her room getting ready, so I hadn't seen what she was wearing yet.

The doorbell rang right as I was tying up my long braid. I peeked out the window and saw Ameerah walking through our lawn. She was dressed in a casual t-shirt and jeans, and I was suddenly feeling way too over-dressed in my long pink top and fancy white and silver skirt. I was just about to check out my closet for something else to wear when I heard my mom call me from downstairs.

"Hanaan! Rahima! They're here! Come downstairs right now!"

I frowned and grumpily headed to greet the guests. As I stepped down the stairs, Rahima came floating past me, descending the staircase before Baba opened the front door to welcome the Sallehs. I caught a quick glimpse of Rahima before she disappeared at the end of the hall. She was wearing an attractive floral dress with a flowy cardigan and a cream-colored silk hijab that framed her glowing face.

The fact that she looked stunning annoyed me more than the fact that she had just ignored me again. How could The Guy resist marrying Rahima when she looked like that?

I tried not to roll my eyes as the parents and the soon-to-be-wed greeted each other in sickly sweet tones. My mom beckoned for me to join the women in the living room and suddenly, I found myself in a tight embrace as Aunty Raabiyah put her arms around me.

"Assalamu alaikum, Hanaan!"

"Wa alaikumussalam," I replied, trying to be polite and masking my annoyance that she was acting like we knew each other so well. "Masha Allah, you are looking so well today. Your braid is so beautiful. Did your sister braid your hair for you?"

I almost snorted at that. Not only was Rahima awful at

hair-dos, but also considering that the two of us were not exactly on speaking terms made that a very unlikely possibility.

"Rahima?" I blurted out. "She's hopeless at doing hair! The last time I asked her to braid my hair…well, I won't be doing that again any time soon."

"Well, I wouldn't go as far as 'hopeless,' but I'm not a hairdresser, that's for sure," Rahima smiled as we all sat down.

"I should say she's not a hairdresser!" I exclaimed, the words escaping my lips before I could stop them. "She chops off her hair every few months just because she doesn't know what to do with it."

"Well," Ameerah's mom said, a bit taken aback. "I like to keep my hair short, too. And so does Ameerah…"

"Yes, well…"

My mom interrupted me with a nervous chuckle. "Hanaan hates to cut her hair, as you can probably tell."

Rahima stood up. "What would you like to drink? Lemonade? Juice?"

"Lemonade would be lovely," Aunty Raabiyah smiled. Rahima turned to Ameerah, who was sitting quietly at the farthest end of the room. "Lemonade, Ameerah?"

Ameerah shook her head. "No, thanks," she said.

"Juice?"

"No."

Rahima didn't push her and headed out of the room. At the doorway, she turned back, almost as an afterthought, and said, "Hanaan, some help?" I couldn't very well refuse her with my mom and the guests right there, so I stood up and followed her.

She walked quickly through the hall, the fabric of her dress swishing in the silence, and didn't say a word until we had reached the kitchen. As soon as we entered the kitchen, she whirled around and grabbed me by the arm, hissing into my ear, "What is *wrong* with you?"

"What do you mean?" Her furious tone startled me into breaking my vow of silence. Rahima never got angry with me, but I had apparently just crossed the wrong line.

"How could you say those things to Abdel-Hakeem's mom?"

"What did I...?"

"I'm hopeless at doing your hair? I chop off my hair because I don't know what to do with it?" Rahima's glare was unnerving.

"It's not like I lied," I defended myself, even though hearing my words again were causing me to cringe with guilt.

"It's not like you lied, huh? Well, you know what, Hanaan? I..."

Someone behind me cleared his throat and Rahima looked up. When she saw who it was, she loosened her hold on my arm and crossed her arms across her chest.

"Are you looking for something?" she asked in a voice that was not her own.

The person behind me chuckled and answered in a deep voice, "Just wanted to wash my hands. Is that allowed here?"

"Yes, it is," Rahima replied. "But I would recommend going to the bathroom for that. It's the second door on the left."

"Ahh, I see. Well, thank you." But the person didn't leave,

and Rahima didn't change her position. My curiosity got the better of me, and I peeked behind me.

I knew right away it was The Guy. I tried to force away the immediate thought that he looked exactly like the kind of guy I would imagine Rahima marrying. *He's so ugly!* I tried to convince myself.

"Well, Heema, aren't you going to introduce us?" he asked, looking at me.

Now I was furious. I was hating my sister right now, but no one could call her "Heema" except for me.

"I don't think RA-hima would like that very much," I replied for her, emphasizing the first syllable of her name.

"Is that so, RA-hima?" Abdel-Hakeem copied my tone perfectly with a smirk.

"I don't appreciate this conversation very much," Rahima said as she turned to take out the lemonade from the fridge.

"Well, then, I guess I'll just have to meet your elusive sister who doesn't want to be introduced some other time."

"I guess so." Rahima was now pouring the lemonade into two glasses, her back turned to the both of us. Abdel-Hakeem winked at me and left the kitchen without another word. Rahima didn't say anything else to me, either. She took the glasses of lemonade and headed back to the living room. I hastily reached for a stack of napkins and followed her.

The two moms were deep in a conversation about their own weddings when we returned to the living room. Out of the corner of my eye, I could see Ameerah tugging at her curly hair. She looked bored out of her mind. Unfortunately for me, my mom

noticed her, too.

"Hanaan, why don't you take Ameerah to your room? The two of you can get to know each other better if you're alone."

My heart sank. I had no interest in being alone for the next few hours with Ameerah again. I tried to catch my mom's attention and plead with my eyes, but she didn't look at me. Instead, she turned to Ameerah and I listened, horrified, as she said, "Hanaan can show you her Fajr's Reflection."

Ameerah looked at me quizzically, and I wished the ground would just swallow me up. Firstly, my mom had insulted my precious place by butchering its name. And secondly, she had suggested that I show it to this girl who clearly didn't like me. What could be worse?

And then, my mom added, "Hanaan likes to write on the roof after Fajr."

This time, Ameerah said something. "On the roof?"

I bit my lip hard. *She probably thinks I'm some sort of hippie now.*

"She'll tell you all about it in her room," my mom said, nudging me to go upstairs.

I beckoned Ameerah to follow me as I led her to my room. "Do you really write on the roof after Fajr?" she asked me incredulously once we were seated in my room.

"No," I said. "I mean, yeah I do, but not on the roof-roof."

"Woah." Her mouth was twitching and I knew she was making fun of me. "So, like, do you use paint or crayons or what?"

"Crayons? What are you talking about?" And then I realized that Ameerah had taken my mom's words literally.

"I don't write on the roof itself, but I do my writing while sitting on the roof," I explained. I didn't know what was going on in Ameerah's head, but I wanted to set her straight.

"Oh, okay."

"Yeah…"

She looked around my room, her gaze pausing at my many books on the shelf next to my bed and my desk next to the window. "But what do you write?"

"It depends on my mood." I felt a sharp pang of pain as I remembered my poem about betrayal flying away from me the other day.

"Writing is basically my worst subject," Ameerah said.

"Yeah, I guess some people feel that way," I replied. "But when you're sitting in the breeze as the sun rises and words just flow onto your paper, it's hard not to love writing, you know?"

Ameerah stared at me blankly. "Nah, can't really relate."

"No, I didn't expect you to."

She turned away from me and I watched as her gaze rested on the blue frame on the wall directly opposite my bed.

"The two lights," she read aloud. I clenched my fist hard, hoping against hope that she wouldn't ask about the story behind the words. "Hey, I think I know that hadith. It's a hadith, right?"

"Yes," I said shortly, fighting against the memories that threatened to flood my mind. Needing something to do, I turned around and determinedly shut the door.

But for some reason, Ameerah really wanted to enlighten me on her Islamic knowledge. "The hadith is something about Surah Fatiha and a door being opened, right?"

I nodded and tightly held onto the doorknob, refusing to

let go, willing the memories away, but it was no use. The image of a younger Rahima materialized into my mind. She was smiling knowingly at me, holding a mysteriously wrapped package in her hands.

I sighed, giving up and letting the memories flow naturally. Even though it had been nearly four years ago, I remembered every detail of that morning.

It was early. The sun had barely risen. I was sitting on the bench swing, furiously swinging back and forth with surprising strength for an eight-year-old. My face was pressed in a determined frown; today Rahima was leaving for her first day of college, and I wasn't ready. I wasn't ready for her to leave me for almost an entire day. What would I do without her?

"Hanaan," my sister's voice called from nearby.

I swung harder, making the swing creak louder and louder to block out anymore sounds. I wanted her to know how sad I was feeling. How betrayed I felt about her leaving. I didn't feel like talking to her right now.

"I have something for you, Hanaan," Rahima said a little more loudly.

The creaking slowed to a stop. I glanced my sister's way, my curiosity getting the better of me. She was holding a package in her hands as she walked determinedly in my direction. *What's that?* I wondered, stepping down from the swing and watching Rahima approach me.

"This is for you," Rahima announced with a witty grin. "The wrapping is a bit off, but it's what's inside that's important."

She handed the package to me. "Oh, and be careful. It's

kinda fragile."

Questions filling my mind, I took the package. I set it down on the bench swing and began tearing away at the brown paper. Upon unwrapping it, my fingertips brushed smooth glass. *Glass?* I wondered, glancing quizzically at my sister.

"It's fine. Open it!" she said giddily.

The paper made a fuzzy sound as I tore the rest of it away. The first thing I saw was a flash of bright blue and then bold curvy letters forming English and Arabic words. A burst of sunlight reflected against the glass of the frame I suddenly realized I was holding and overpowered my eyes. I held the frame up against the sunlight so I could read what was written on it.

"It's the story about the two lights," Rahima softly explained to me as comprehension began to dawn on my face. "Remember when I was telling you about it? That Allah sent down two lights from the same door in Jannah that had never been opened before? Surah Fatiha and — "

"The last two ayahs of Surah Baqarah," I finished for her, remembering that warm feeling I initially had when hearing about the miracle of those sections of the Qur'an.

Rahima smiled as she gently took the frame from my hand and placed it down on the bench swing so I would turn all my attention to her as she spoke. "That's what I want you to remember, that even when I'm not here, you will always have someone to turn to. Allah always knows when you're feeling sad. Whenever you're missing me, just think that Allah knows exactly what you and I are thinking, and that He's watching both of us at the same exact time. Okay?"

I nodded, unable to form any words to express how much I loved my sister at that moment. And then, she was hugging me only as Rahima could. I didn't want to let go. I didn't want this moment to end. Rahima held onto me, and I knew she wouldn't be the first one to let go. I breathed in my sister's scent, pondering over the changes that today would bring. Rahima was only going off to college. She would still be home at night and on the weekends. She still loved me and would never forget about me. I glanced at the frame on the swing and felt reassured. I was going to be okay.

I let go of my sister and stepped back, feeling warm and loved. As she got into her car and began backing out of the driveway, her windows rolled down, I waved enthusiastically and yelled, "Have fun in college!" The image that remained in my mind for the rest of the day was her beaming smile as she drove off, leaving me to hug the frame to my chest.

"What a pretty border."

Ameerah's voice broke into my thoughts. I glanced around, slowly adapting back to the present. My gaze landed on Ameerah. The girl was standing in front of my frame. She slowly reached out a hand.

No! I wasn't about to let her soil my frame. I swiftly stepped forward to get in front of Ameerah. She looked up at me, confusion in her eyes.

"Please don't touch that," I said, trying my best not to be rude.

"Why?"

"Because...well, it's just kind of important, that's all." I was struggling to stay patient.

Ameerah gave me a weird look, but she stepped back. "Okay. I'm sorry."

I said nothing for a moment and motioned for Ameerah to go back to my bed. She stared at my frame for a long moment, her eyebrows creased as if she were confused. Finally, with a flip of her brown curls, she sat back on my bed and studied my bookshelves. "That's a lot of books," she commented. She hesitated for a moment and then said, "You're homeschooled, right?"

The question annoyed me. The girl knew I was homeschooled. We had just had a whole conversation about it at her house, for crying out loud.

"Yeah, I am," I said.

She obviously didn't take the hint because her next question was, "So that's just, like, doing school, but at your house?"

"Well, yeah, you could say that," I replied, struggling to keep the sarcasm at bay. "Homeschooling usually is school done at home." She seemed a bit taken aback by my response, which made me feel a bit guilty. "But I don't do everything at home. I have a tutor I visit most days and a homeschool group I meet with once a week."

"So your parents aren't your only teachers?"

"No."

"Oh."

We were both quiet for a few moments, looking around and refusing to meet each other's gaze. And then...

"So you still get to hang out and study with friends?"

I was startled to find that there was a hint of pleading in Ameerah's voice. I had assumed that she thought that homeschooling was for weirdos and that she was bitter about it. But now it sounded like she was just worried about being lonely. I imagined that Ameerah was used to socializing with lots of friends in school and on the basketball court. It seemed like she was afraid all of that would end once she started homeschooling.

I smiled reassuringly at her and said, "Of course I do! And my schedule is a lot more flexible since I'm homeschooled so I get to do lots of things during the day that many other kids can't."

She tilted her head and squinted at me. "Like what?"

"Literally anything. I can go to the park or the flower garden or a museum when it's less crowded."

Ameerah laughed. I wrinkled my forehead in confusion. "Sorry, I'm not laughing at you." She laughed again. "I've always wanted to skip school one day and go to the roller skating rink when it's not crowded. I tried to convince my brother to take me once, but my mom wouldn't let us."

"Maybe she will let you now that you're going to start homeschooling."

Ameerah looked thoughtful. "Maybe."

She didn't seem as pessimistic about the idea as she was earlier. It seemed that, somehow, I was slowly changing her impression of homeschooling. And, somehow, this evening wasn't turning out as badly as I thought it would be.

Chapter 16
Ameerah

An awkward silence filled the room. For once, I didn't know what to say, especially after that conversation about homeschooling. I hadn't realized that homeschooling had cool parts, too. My head was jumbled up with all the new ideas Hanaan had put in there. Trying to shake them away, I bared my teeth and ran my tongue over them.

"Is purple your favorite color?" Hanaan asked.

"Yeah," I replied, giving her a suspicious side glance. "How did you guess?"

Hanaan shrugged. "I could kind of tell. I remember that your room was purple, the T-shirt you're wearing right now is purple, and your braces are purple."

Dang, this girl is observant. "Oh, I see. Yeah, I suppose I made it kind of obvious," I said. "What about you?" Nodding at her pink top, I said, "Is it pink? You seem to have a lot of pink clothes."

She gave a small smile. "My favorite color is actually mint green, but pink is a good guess. It's my mom's favorite color, so she always wants to buy me pink things."

"Woah." Pink did not seem like a mom color to me, but maybe that was just because my mom never wore pink. I began looking around her room again to figure out something else to say. I noticed the picture frame for the second time. Hanaan hadn't said much about it, and I felt like there was more to the frame than what met the eye. What did it mean? And why was she so against me touching it?

I tried to catch her eye to ask another question about it, but before I could open my mouth, I heard Aunty Nusaybah's voice calling from downstairs. "Hanaan! It's time to eat."

Hanaan jerked her head towards the door. "Come on," she said, rising from her chair.

I followed closely behind her on the stairs, the conversations from below getting louder as we descended. Upon reaching the bottom of the stairs, I could distinctly hear Hanaan's mother saying, "Do you think they're getting along?"

Who? I wondered as we reached the kitchen. Rahima, who sat at one end of the dining table, was the first to see us. She smiled brightly and waved at us. "There they are!" she said cheerfully.

Oh. Hanaan and I. Duh.

Our mothers, who had their backs turned to us, turned around as Rahima spoke. When we reached the table, they looked at us with huge grins on their faces. "There you are!" Mama said. "Are you girls enjoying yourselves?"

Hanaan didn't say anything, so I replied, "Her room is like a *library!*"

I wasn't trying to be funny, but for some reason, everybody laughed. "Hanaan does love her books," Aunty Nusaybah chuckled. "Do you like to read, as well, Ameerah?"

I shook my head. "Not really."

"Oh, my Ameerah is all about sports," said Mama. "You should see her room. It's practically a trophy museum in there!"

I couldn't find the lie in Mama's words, so I just nodded.

"Oh, how nice!" Aunty Nusaybah remarked. "You should come over sometime, Ameerah, and teach Hanaan to play some sports. That sounds fun, doesn't it, Hanaan?"

We all turned to look at Hanaan. She looked like she wanted to say no, but she said, "Maybe."

I noticed Aunty Nusaybah and Rahima exchange looks. It was kind of obvious that Hanaan and I still weren't too enthusiastic about hanging out with each other.

My stomach growled suddenly.

Rahima and our mothers laughed, seemingly relieved about having an escape from the awkward atmosphere. "I guess it's time to eat, huh?" Aunty Nusaybah said. She gestured toward the food. "Here. You two can start us off."

After taking our food, Hanaan and I took our seats at the table. Hanaan sat at one end of the table, and I sat opposite her. Rahima took the seat to my right. Hoping I would finally get a break from all this forced conversation, I scooped up some rice from my plate. It worked out that Hanaan sat across from me at the very end of the table, so it wouldn't be easy for me to talk to her. Silently satisfied at the idea of no longer having to talk with basically strangers for the rest of the night, I began to savor the sweet silence and brought my spoon to my mouth.

Breaking into my moment of silence suddenly, Rahima asked me, "How old are you, Ameerah?"

Proved wrong. I spooned all the rice into my mouth and finished taking it down before answering, "I'm eleven."

"Oh my goodness! Hanaan is eleven too! She turns twelve next month, on the same day I turn 22. Did you know we shared a birthday?"

"Oh, nice. No, I didn't," I said, my mouth full of rice. *But I guess that's cool? Why should I care?*

"I thought you always bragged about it to your friends, Hanaan," Rahima said, addressing her sister.

Friends? Hanaan and I slid questioning glances to each other. *Are we friends?* The thought quickly vanished when I saw the similar question spread across Hanaan's face.

Rahima didn't bother to hide a grin and then asked me, "So, when are you turning twelve?"

"My birthday is August 1st." I chewed on more rice. *This tastes pretty good, actually.*

"Oh, that's a nice birthday!" Rahima answered. "You open up the whole month of August for everyone, huh?"

"Yeah, I guess so," I replied, cracking a small smile.

Rahima then nudged me from a different direction. "What sports do you play?"

"Basketball," I answered immediately. "I've been on a basketball team every year since I was in elementary school. I started archery in third grade, and I take taekwondo. Also, I like to run around my neighborhood and I roller blade sometimes. And my brother Ali and I like to exercise together."

"Woah!" Rahima chuckled. Across from the table, Hanaan calmly ate her lasagna, but I could tell she was listening to our conversation.

"Abdel-Hakeem told me you were a sports fanatic."

"What else did he tell you?" I asked.

She grinned. "All good things, don't worry," she said with a wink. "Y'all like to have ice cream at Polar Point, right?"

I nodded. "I always order orange sorbet topped with strawberry cheesecake in a chocolate waffle cone."

"What?" Hanaan shot a wide-eyed look at me.

Rahima's eyes bugged out. "No way!" she exclaimed. "That's Hanaan's favorite, too!"

I glanced at Hanaan. "Really?" I asked hesitantly.

Hanaan was silent for a moment, then slowly nodded. "Yes..."

"Oh my god, that's so cool!" Rahima squealed, clasping her hands. "For the longest time I thought Hanaan was the only person in the world who liked that combination!"

"Yeah... it is pretty unique," I said. I thought back to all the times Sherine had teased me for mixing together some of the weirdest flavors of ice cream. Come to think of it, the rest of my team had made fun of me as well. Their comments never really affected me that much, but I'd always wanted to know someone who didn't think I was a weirdo when it came to ice cream flavors.

But Rahima wasn't finished with us. "Dude, Hanaan, Ameerah's like your soul sister!"

Uh, soul sisters? No.

"Ice cream preference is hardly a contributing factor to soul sisterhood," Hanaan said suddenly.

While I tried to wrap my head around what she had just said, Rahima turned back to me. "So, what else do you do other than sports?"

"I like to watch documentaries," I replied.

"Ooh, cool! On what?"

"History, mostly."

Hanaan looked at me again and narrowed her eyes.

I couldn't contain my curiosity. "Does Hanaan like history too?

"She does!" Rahima said with a laugh. "But she prefers to read it instead of watching it."

"Oh," I said. "I thought so. It's easier for me to remember things when I watch them, though."

"Ahh, so you're a visual person." Rahima nodded.

"Yup."

Finally, the night was over, and we could go home. "Let me know when you try out that recipe," Mama said to Aunty Nusaybah as they hugged.

"For sure! I'm excited to try it," Aunty Nusaybah replied. "Oh, and send me the link to that nasheed you mentioned."

"Insha Allah," Mama said with a laugh. She turned to me. "Ameerah, say salam, will you?"

I held out my hand to Aunty Nusaybah, who shook it with a smile. "See you soon, dear," she said. "I think Hanaan likes you very much."

I raised my eyebrows. *Hmm. Maybe.* I then moved on to Rahima.

"I loved talking with you!" she said, smiling. "See you at the wedding, insha Allah!"

I nodded and smiled back. "Yeah. Insha Allah." By now my family was walking out of the house, and as I followed them, I looked back at Hanaan. I didn't know why, but something was telling me to wave at her. And maybe Hanaan was simply pushing wisps of hair behind her ear, but I was positive she waved back.

Chapter 17
Hanaan

I snapped a tiny green puzzle piece into the center of an image of a blooming peach tree. I was trying to put together a 500-piece puzzle on the coffee table in the living room to keep my mind off things. I enjoyed concentrating on a puzzle and slowly putting it together as an image began to form. This particular puzzle was a large circle divided up into four separate parts, one for each season. I had already finished winter and was in the middle of the spring section.

My face scrunched up in concentration, I almost didn't notice Rahima enter the living room. Almost.

Out of the corner of my eye, I saw her hesitate before approaching the sofa I was sitting on.

"Hey," she said.

"Hey," I replied without looking up. I had already broken my vow of silence yesterday, so it was pointless to ignore her anymore.

"Cool puzzle," she said, waving her hand over the portion I had already completed as she sat down beside me.

"Thanks," I grunted.

"Can I help?"

Rahima hated puzzles as a rule, so this was a bit unexpected, but I moved over to give her room. "Sure."

For a few minutes, we sat in silence. I could tell Rahima wasn't really into it because she kept picking up random puzzle pieces and putting them back down. I wasn't progressing much either, since I was now in the midst of trying to put together the sky.

"How do you even do the sky when all the pieces are the same color?" Rahima asked, watching me sort through the puzzle pieces to find all the sky blue ones.

"They're different shades of blue. And each piece is a different shape, so you can just tell which ones go together and which ones don't."

"Dude, the pieces are so tiny, though."

"Yeah, well…" I let my statement drift off into the air because I had just been about to playfully tease her like I normally did. How was it that even though we hadn't talked together in weeks, it was so easy to just pick up a normal conversation again?

"Oh my goodness, though, Hanaan. You know who texted me this morning?"

"Who?"

"Rachel from ECON 101! Remember I told you about that class I took back in my first year?"

"The one with the professor whose voice sounded like a frog?" I couldn't stop myself from smiling at the memory.

"Yes, exactly! And did I ever tell you what Rachel and I used to do?"

"You took turns going to class and taking notes for each other, right?"

"Yesss! It was the best because I only had to go to class half the time."

"And the professor didn't even notice because the class was so big."

"Yeah…those were the days…" Rahima was looking out into space with a dreamy expression on her face.

"Well?"

Rahima snapped back to attention. "Hmm?"

"You were saying Rachel texted you?"

"Oh yeah, she heard that I was getting married so she wanted to congratulate me."

"Oh." I went back to concentrating extra hard on the puzzle. I had no interest in talking about Rahima getting married right now.

"Wasn't that nice of her?"

"I guess."

Noticing that I was no longer enjoying the conversation, Rahima turned back to the puzzle, too.

Having set aside the sky for a bit, I pushed together another bunch of flowers into my peach tree and then realized I only needed one piece left to finish the tree. I scanned the table for a bright peach-colored puzzle piece, but it was nowhere in sight. Sifting through some red puzzle pieces at the far end of the table with no success, I was momentarily confused. Then, I saw that Rahima was absently fiddling with a puzzle piece in her hand.

"Can I see that?" I reached for the piece in her hand. "Aha! I've been looking for this. You're not helping by playing with the puzzle pieces, you know."

"Oh, sorry." Rahima handed me the piece and tapped a little rhythm on the table with her fingers. "It's kinda hot in here, don't you think?"

"Mmm, I guess." I triumphantly completed my peach tree

and set to work on the next plant.

Rahima picked up another puzzle piece, and fingering a few strands of her shoulder-length hair, she said teasingly, "I guess it's too bad I'm hopeless at doing hair. Otherwise, I might have been able to do something with this."

Is she seriously going to talk about this right now? I thought to myself.

When I didn't say anything, Rahima nudged me. "Hmm, Hanaan? Isn't that right?"

I avoided her gaze. "Maybe."

Then, Rahima's voice took on a serious tone. "Hey, about yesterday?"

My heart rate increased slightly.

"I didn't mean to get so mad at you, okay?"

"Well, I *was* telling the truth."

"You were."

"And you've always said to tell the truth."

"Yes, I have."

"And you've also said it's important to be able to control your anger."

"Yes, I've said that, too."

"So you really shouldn't have gotten mad at me."

"No, I shouldn't have."

"You were contradicting yourself."

"Maybe so."

"But you've also said to keep silent if you have nothing good to say."

"I...yes, I did."

"So I shouldn't have said what I did, either."

"No, you shouldn't have." Rahima stopped her pretense of doing the puzzle and looked at me. "Hanaan, can't we talk about the wedding?"

"No," I replied.

"But do you forgive me?"

I knew she wasn't just talking about yesterday, and as I looked into my sister's eyes, I knew I wasn't mad at her anymore.

I nodded and quickly looked away.

"Then that's good enough for now." She stood up and squeezed my shoulder affectionately before heading out of the living room. "I'm meeting with Kathy in a bit. Sure you don't want to join us?"

"Quite sure."

"Okay, suit yourself. Honestly, how do you sit for hours over that thing?"

"It's called a puzzle."

"I know what it's called, thank you very much." And she left the living room with a spirited laugh and an extra spring in her step.

The doorbell rang right when I was connecting the spring and winter sections of my puzzle together. Startled by the sound, I nearly slid a large portion of the puzzle right off the table. Luckily, I caught it with my arm just in time.

Rahima and Kathy, the wedding planner, entered the room to see me crouched in an awkward position with my right arm balancing my puzzle and my legs crossed over each other around the table.

"Woah, is this puzzle-making gymnastics now?" Rahima teased as she headed to the adjoining dining room with Kathy in tow.

I shot her a dirty look without saying anything and attempted to untangle myself.

"My sister has a knack for things like puzzles," I heard Rahima say as she took a seat at the dining table beside the wedding planner.

"I used to like puzzles, too, when I was little," Kathy replied in a too-bright airy voice, smiling at me. I rolled my eyes when she turned around. The girl wasn't much older than me, but she was acting like I was some little kid.

"Okay then, Rahima, I just have a few things I have to go over with you before the big day."

I groaned inwardly, realizing that I would literally be hearing their entire conversation from my position in the living room. Struggling to block out their voices, I directed my attention to my puzzle, picking up a piece that looked like it belonged to the summer section.

"The reservation for the venue is all set. All that's left for that is the payment. You can just give me the cash, and I'll make out a check to Tres Belle Hotel so you won't have to worry about it."

I tried to connect two puzzle pieces together to form a tree branch, but they didn't fit. Tossing one of the pieces aside, I searched for another possible match.

"And about the flowers. I can pick them up at Botanica the day before the reception and bring them over to the hall."

"That would be great, Kathy. And I also wanted to know about the centerpieces. Are they going to be the ones in the picture you emailed me the other day?"

Furious, I threw down my puzzle piece with such force that a few pieces popped up like hot corn kernels and teetered dangerously on the edge of the table. I didn't care. *I can't listen to another moment of this wedding talk,* I thought through gritted teeth, and I angrily made my way out of the room, pushing away a nagging thought in my mind that something, somehow, was a bit out of place. I'd forgiven my sister, all right, but only for her mistake in not notifying me of the biggest change of her life. The upcoming wedding was still an issue, and I could not, no matter how hard I tried, feel happy about it.

Chapter 18
Ameerah

"Kathy said she reserved a room for us in the Tres Belle hotel," Abdel-Hakeem said. "She did say there would be another event taking up the other two ballrooms, but they wouldn't bother us."

Mama's brows furrowed. "The other two ballrooms?" she asked anxiously. "Are you sure they won't bother us? Will we even have enough space for all the guests?"

I chewed on my soggy corn flakes, annoyed that I had to eat breakfast while having to listen to Abdel-Hakeem talk about his wedding. It was the last thing I wanted to talk about. Or hear about, since I'd never really engaged in any conversation concerning the wedding.

Before I had to listen to anything else, I left the table and let my bowl and spoon clatter in the sink. Then, I hurried upstairs to my room. Rain fell in sheets outside once more, so I was stuck inside the dark house with my mother and brothers. Baba was not home because he had worked a night shift right after leaving Hanaan's house yesterday. Someone needed to have surgery done on their knee. It was an ACL tear, Mama had said, and boy, I knew everything I wanted to know about ACL tears. A few years back, Ali had torn his ligament during a game of soccer, and I had been so worried about him that I pleaded to join him in the surgery room. Of course, I was not allowed to in the end, but when the surgery was finally over, I had to watch Ali walk on crutches for several weeks before he could play soccer again.

Ali! I suddenly realized I was randomly thinking about him again. And how he'd been too busy to spend time with me. He was growing so distant from me that I was getting a little worried. And I wasn't about to let him forget me so easily. *I wonder if he's in his room right now. I'm gonna go see.* I headed for his room and held up my hand to knock, but the door was already open. That meant Ahmed wasn't in. Cautiously, I peeked inside.

"Ali?" I called.

The room was darker than the house already was. Slowly, I stepped inside. The only things I could see were the orange and green lights flickering on Ahmed's gaming computer. The curtain of the window at the end of the room was open just a tad, letting a thin line of gray light run across Ali's bed. A laptop sat open on the bed, the screen black. It flickered every so often with white words floating around on the screen.

The odor of socks and dried orange rinds hung in the air from Ahmed's side of the room, and I pinched my nose as I advanced to Ali's side, which always smelled, looked, and felt better than Ahmed's. It was a bummer I had to walk through Ahmed's side to get to Ali's.

"Ali," I whisper-shouted. I didn't know why I felt the need to whisper, but being in the dark made me feel trapped. Where was the light switch?

Ali's laptop flickered again, and I hurried over to it, desperate for a source of light. The laptop's light sent a glow onto the bedspread, exposing the empty bed. Ali was not in the room.

Nevertheless, I crawled into Ali's bed and moved the mouse to awaken his laptop. What was he so busy with, I wondered, that he didn't have time for me anymore? The screen lit up, causing my eyes to burn. I lowered the screen brightness as far as it could go, then studied what was on the screen. An art program was open, showing a huge, brightly colored poster on the display. In giant block letters on the front were the words, "Big German Festival!"

German festival. Interesting. I read on.

Where: Tres Belle Hotel

When: Saturday, June 21st

ALL THREE BALLROOMS ARE RESERVED FOR THIS EVENT.

I raised my eyebrows. *Wait a second. All three ballrooms?* What was that Abdel-Hakeem had said at breakfast? "Kathy said she reserved a room for us in the Tres Belle hotel. She did say there would be another event taking up the other two ballrooms, but they wouldn't bother us."

Another event taking up the other two ballrooms. I read over the information again. June 21st? Wait a second. I'd heard that date before. Hadn't Rahima mentioned something about that when she'd come over? I remembered her saying something about the wedding being on the weekend of the 21st. I remembered that easily, because I could recall being super annoyed when the moms were showing each other their phone calendars and talking non-stop about the wedding. It was like there was nothing else to talk about.

"We'd like to have at least a week to get settled into our new home before Ramadan starts. So we were thinking the weekend of the 21st," Rahima had said.

My heart skipped a beat. Every detail Rahima had listed

was right before my eyes. And on *Ali's* computer! Didn't he know what he was doing?

Before I could think about what I was doing, I pulled up a web browser and searched "Tres Belle Hotel." Instantly, results popped up, asking to book a room or to reserve a ballroom. I clicked on the website for the hotel and scrolled through the page, until I found a link that said, "Upcoming Events." On that page was a list of events for all of June, and as I read each one, my heart rate increased.

JUNE 10: BIRTHDAY PARTY (PRIVATE EVENT)

JUNE 14-16: SINGLE-WEEKEND SEMINAR (PRIVATE EVENT)

JUNE 21: GERMAN FESTIVAL (PUBLIC EVENT)

JUNE 28-30: YOUTH GROUP CONFERENCE

Oh no. The Tres Belle Hotel was basically being used for the entire month of June! There was no space for my brother's wedding! *But then, why would they schedule their wedding for June 21st, and not any other day?* I wondered. *Their wedding planner should have known about this!*

An idea sparked in my mind. *Unless the wedding planner is doing this on purpose.*

I instantly felt an impulse to hightail downstairs and tell Abdel-Hakeem what I'd found, when the overhead light in the room suddenly turned on.

I whipped my head upwards.

"Ameerah! What are you doing here?" came Ali's voice, getting louder the closer he approached me.

"Ali!" I said, glad to see him. "I just found—"

"Why are you on my laptop?" Ali hurried over and turned the laptop to face him. With his hand on the trackpad, his eyes darted rapidly around the screen. After seemingly checking that everything was okay, he sighed, stood up straight, and looked at me.

"Ameerah, I'm working on important things right now. If anything is messed up, I'll be behind on all the work I need to do. Do you understand?"

I nodded. "Sorry."

"Okay, good." Ali settled himself on his bed in front of his laptop. When I didn't leave, he looked up at me and jutted his chin in the direction of the door.

I took my cue and left the room.

Chapter 19
Hanaan

Rahima's and Kathy's voices faded away as I approached my room upstairs. I tried to block their conversation out of my mind by getting out my origami papers and concentrating on a difficult design, but bits of what they had said kept coming back to me.

There was something about that wedding planner that just didn't sit well with me. At first, I thought it was because I was thinking of her as a symbol of the wedding, and anything that reminded me of the wedding bothered me. But the more I thought about it, there was more to it than simply what Kathy represented. Was it her too-loud voice that made it seem like she was trying extra hard to be authentic? Was it the way she looked at me that made me feel like I was two years old? Or was it something more than that? Something…something else.

I folded a crease a bit severely as I played Kathy's words in my mind over and over again. Tres Belle Hotel…payment…flowers…Botanica…Botanica…

What was it about Botanica that was ringing bells? Why did I feel like I knew something about this? And then, I remembered.

Weddings can be a pretty stressful time, Sr. Jamilah had said only three days ago when she was trying to convince me to cut Rahima some slack. And then she'd told me about the drama surrounding flowers on her own wedding day, how Botanica Flowers wasn't open on Fridays so she had to make different arrangements at the last minute.

But why was this bothering me? And what did it have to do with Kathy? All Kathy had said was that she was going to pick up the flowers the day before the reception from Botanica. So?

I had been deliberately trying to avoid any wedding talk over the past few weeks, but now I found myself desperately trying to remember anything I had heard about the wedding. At Ameerah's house last week, Rahima had said that the reception was set for June 21st, a Saturday.

Ohhhh.

The day before Saturday was a Friday and Botanica wasn't open on Fridays. But what did this mean? Was Kathy lying about getting the flowers? Or did she just not know about the timings? But this was her job. She was supposed to know these details.

That's what she was being paid to do.

I didn't know what to think. What I had just figured out wasn't enough to accuse Kathy of fraud. But there was definitely something going on. And I…

The sound of frantic footsteps on the stairs interrupted my thoughts.

"Hanaan!" I heard Rahima call my name. "Abdel-Hakeem and his mom are stopping by in five minutes. Can you grab my blue cardigan from the laundry room? I gotta change, like, right now."

I popped my head out my door and saw Rahima dash into her room. "Is your cardigan in the dryer?"

"No, it's hanging on top."

"Okay." I headed to the laundry room at the end of the hall, passing the huge floor to ceiling windows down below. I heard a car door slam and caught a glimpse of someone walking up the front path.

"Umm, Rahima?"

"Yeah?"

"Did you say they're coming in five minutes? Because I think they're here now." And just as I said that, the doorbell rang.

"Aah!" I heard Rahima make a frustrated sound followed by a thud that sounded like she had tripped over something. "Can you go open the door, Hanaan? I'm not ready yet."

"Me?"

"How many Hanaans are there around here?"

"What about Mama?"

"She's praying." The doorbell rang again. "Hanaan, please?"

"Okay," I grumbled. It was going to be the most awkward thing ever to open the door for The Guy and his mom, especially after what had happened last time they had come to visit. I reluctantly went down the stairs, descending the steps as slowly as I could.

"Hurry, Hanaan!" Rahima called from her room.

"Okay, okay." I took a deep breath, walked the length of the hall and then opened the front door. To my surprise, the first person I saw wasn't the tall, grinning Abdel-Hakeem or his cheerful, bustling mom; it was a short girl with curly hair and braces.

Rahima didn't say Ameerah was coming, too! I thought furiously.

Aloud, I greeted the trio and asked them to come inside. I avoided looking directly at Ameerah, feeling slightly awkward as I remembered our intense conversation the previous day.

"My mom and Rahima will be here in a minute," I said and led them to the dining room where Kathy was scribbling something in a little notepad.

"Hi!" Kathy said in a voice that was way too loud and cheerful. "How're you doing? I'm Kathy, the wedding planner."

I watched Abdel-Hakeem and his mom warmly greet her back and introduce themselves, but then I noticed Ameerah looking decidedly unimpressed. She had a defiant expression on her face as she stared unblinkingly at Kathy. She grumbled something when her mom introduced her to the wedding planner, and I bit my lip when Kathy took on an extra high-pitched tone.

"Aww, well aren't you the sweetest little thing?"

Ameerah seemed just as outraged as I had been earlier when Kathy had been talking to me, and for the first time, I felt something like a shared moment with the younger girl.

The moment didn't last long. Rahima suddenly appeared, having pulled on a blue dress and the cardigan that I was supposed to have gotten for her. A white hijab was slightly haphazardly wrapped around her head, but her face was glowing so it wasn't really obvious. Greeting the newcomers warmly and embracing Ameerah's mom with a smile, she turned to me and Ameerah.

"We're gonna be talking about wedding prep stuff for a bit. Do you girls wanna join? It's only gonna take a few minutes or so."

"No, thanks," I responded immediately, annoyed that she had grouped me with Ameerah using the words "you girls." It wasn't until everyone else started laughing when I realized that Ameerah had said, "no thanks" at the same exact time.

No one did anything for a moment and Rahima raised her

eyebrows at me, and I knew she was indicating that I should take Ameerah to my room.

"Well, let's go to my room then," I said a bit ungraciously.

"Okay," Ameerah replied, sounding glad to get away, and fell into step behind me. From the hall, I could hear Kathy remarking, "Those two little girls! It's so cute how they're so close in age." I rolled my eyes without bothering to hide my disdain from Ameerah.

"You don't like her, huh?" she asked.

"How could anyone like her?" I responded. Then I realized what I'd just said. "I mean…"

Ameerah stopped me. "Nah, I get you."

I don't know what made me say it. Maybe I just felt like being reckless today, but the next thing I said was, "There's something not right about her, you know. She makes me feel uneasy, and it's not just how she is when she talks to me."

I expected Ameerah to reject my statement or at least look a little surprised, but instead, she nodded at me.

"Same here."

"What?" I asked her incredulously. We had reached my room by now, and I opened the door to let her in. "You just met her, though. You haven't had to endure hearing her have long discussions about wedding planning."

"Yeah, but…" Ameerah stopped.

"But what?" Now I was getting curious. Ameerah had this look in her eye like she was debating whether or not to say something.

"It's probably nothing," she said finally with a toss of her head. She sounded confident, but her wandering gaze told otherwise.

"What's probably nothing?" I was now too curious to be ashamed of asking too many questions.

"Well," Ameerah said hesitantly, then lowered her voice. "I kinda searched up that place. Tres Belle Hotel, right?"

"And?" I prodded her.

"It has three ballrooms that it rents out for events and things, alright?"

"Okay…"

"And I checked what events they have booked for June 21st."

"Okay?"

Ameerah sucked in her breath. "Apparently, all three ballrooms are being rented out for this big German festival that day. It says so right on the website."

I just looked at her, my eyes widening in comprehension. "Kathy didn't really rent out a room for us, did she?"

"Well, no, unless your sister wants to have a German festival on her wedding day."

"Uh…well, no, she doesn't," I said lamely.

"That's what I thought." Ameerah crossed her arms and gave me a look. "Well?"

"Well, what?"

"What about you? Why did you feel like something's wrong with Kathy?"

I hesitated for a moment.

"You *were* saying that she makes you uneasy, right?"

Ameerah rubbed her cheek.

"Yeah, but it's not like something definite," I answered with an annoyed sigh. "It's just how I always just feel like she's trying to be someone she's not. And that's what makes me feel uneasy."

"Is that all?" Ameerah sounded a bit disappointed.

"Well, I did notice that some things just weren't right about the flowers."

Ameerah nodded to indicate she was listening, and then I explained what I had figured out earlier based on Sr. Jamilah's story.

"Woah. That's... deep," she said.

"Of course, my tutor got married a few years ago, so Botanica's timings could have changed," I admitted.

"Maybe..."

We looked at each other for a few moments in silence. I knew we were both thinking, *What now?* The information we had gathered was enough to raise anyone's suspicions, but was it enough to accuse Kathy of being a fraud?

Ameerah stroked my wall. "Well, the wedding is this coming Saturday," she said. She glanced at me. "So, what now?"

"I don't know!" I said, frustrated that she was looking to me for an answer. "I'm just tired of all this wedding stuff!"

"Same," Ameerah agreed with a flip of her curls.

"You?" I asked bitterly. I rounded on her, and she backed away, startled. "You? You have *nothing to lose.* You have a bunch of brothers still at your house to hang out with you. Rahima is my only sibling. With her leaving me, I have no one else. You have no right to complain!"

Ameerah opened her mouth in surprise, but I continued.

"You've never had a sister so you don't know what this feels like and what it means to me." I hurried across the floor, leading Ameerah to the hadith frame hanging on my wall. I thrust a shaking finger at it. "You see this frame over here? This used to mean something to me! This was a gift from *her!* It was a *symbol of our relationship!*"

My voice was on the verge of breaking. I paused my ranting and placed my hands on the table that stood under the frame, bending over so that Ameerah couldn't see my face. Tears smarted at my eyes, but I held them back. And then, in a sudden surge of anger, I slapped the table with both my hands. Hard.

The hadith frame teetered back and forth on the wall. I glanced up at it, my mouth open. *Don't fall. Don't break,* I silently begged the frame. I backed away and found myself edging closer to Ameerah. We both watched, tense, as the frame swayed once more, then landed on the table. My eyes shut tight, I cringed as I anticipated the familiar sound of glass breaking. But all I heard was a loud thud.

For a moment, Ameerah and I remained silent. Then, I opened my eyes and inched forward to inspect the frame. It wasn't completely shattered, but there was a giant crack down the front of it. Slowly, I extended my hand and ran my finger down the crack. "I guess that's what's become of your relationship now," Ameerah commented, breaking the silence.

I sucked my lips inward and gave the frame a rough push against the wall. This time, the sound of glass breaking rang out sharply as the crack widened and separated into shards.

I guess that's what's become of your relationship now, echoed Ameerah's words in my mind.

Ameerah took a few steps back. "I... I'm sorry, Hanaan," she whispered hoarsely.

I didn't say anything. I avoided her gaze.

"Well..." Ameerah cleared her throat. "What do we do? What do you think we should do?"

"About what?" My voice came out in a gruff, defeated tone.

"Should we tell them about Kathy? Or let the wedding get ruined?"

Every word she said felt like an individual weight on my ears. *Let the wedding get ruined?*

"Everything is already ruined," I said bitterly, emphasizing on each word.

Ameerah hesitated. I still wasn't meeting her gaze, but I could tell she was on the verge of saying something. But at that moment, Rahima called to me from downstairs. "Hanaan! Ameerah's leaving now."

I stood up straight. "Coming!" I nodded to Ameerah and the two of us hurried downstairs, just in time to see Kathy slide into her way-too-tall high heels.

"It was great talking with you guys today!" she was saying airily.

"Yes, it was nice meeting you!" Ameerah's mom replied. The door closed behind Kathy with a thud, leaving Rahima, Abdel-Hakeem and Aunty Raabiyah standing by the shoe rack. They noticed us once we reached the bottom of the staircase.

"I told you that was going to be quick," Abdel-Hakeem

grinned at Ameerah. She met his gaze with a frown, but remained silent. I shot her an expectant look, waiting for her to say something about Kathy, but she didn't catch my eye.

"It's good you have Kathy to prepare the whole wedding reception," Aunty Raabiyah said to Rahima. "That way you two can concentrate more on the move."

"Yeah, I really haven't had to worry about the wedding at all so far, alhamdulillah," Rahima replied.

I tried again to look at Ameerah, but I couldn't read her expression. Was she going to say something about Kathy or not? Besides, she was the one who'd brought it up.

"Did you guys get to talk about anything interesting?" Rahima asked, turning to me and Ameerah.

If there was ever a time to say anything, now would be it, but somehow my mouth couldn't move around the words.
"It sure was an enlightening conversation," Ameerah answered for me with a slight smile, eyeing me when she did. I quickly nodded in agreement.

"Well, that sounds like progress," Aunty Raabiyah chuckled. Rahima and Abdel-Hakeem grinned as the three Sallehs exited the house in a flurry of cheerful salams. I caught a glimpse of Ameerah staring at me just before the front door closed. We were now bound by our shared secret, and only time would tell whether we would reveal it or not.

Chapter 20
Ameerah

Everything Hanaan had said was lingering in my mind like the smell of paint in a new house. The timings for Botanica. That Kathy lady trying to be someone she wasn't. Her frame that symbolized her relationship with her sister. After connecting this information to what I had discovered, everything was beginning to make sense. But I needed more proof.

In the days that followed since Hanaan and I had confided in each other, I deliberately yet subtly tried to listen in on any conversation concerning the wedding. Whenever Abdel-Hakeem talked about it during mealtime, I ate much more slowly than I usually did. If Mama and Abdel-Hakeem were nearby talking about wedding plans, I would immediately stop where I was and start practicing my taekwondo katas. And when Abdel-Hakeem was talking to someone on the phone, I would sit nearby with Ali's iPad, watching food videos like I typically did, but while actually patiently listening to every second of his conversation. My patience in trying to obtain any extra information turned out to be mostly fruitless, because all I discovered were useless things like the bride's dress color or the types of food that was going to be served on the big day. However, there were a few bits of information I did find interesting, which made all my hard work worth it.

Trying to get Ali's attention had been pushed to the back of my mind, as I was finally occupied with something else. Something much more interesting. I had not asked Ali about this flyer he was making, and didn't yet plan to. He was so busy everyday with work and took a nap right after he came home, then stayed up late at night to work on some work project. He barely had any free time. It wasn't just me he was abandoning. It was the whole family. And that must have been why he hadn't realized that the German festival clashed with Abdel-Hakeem's wedding.

One morning, I was walking outside in our backyard garden, which to me felt a lot more like a vegetable forest. In one bed, stalks of corn shot higher than the fence surrounding the yard. Next door in a smaller bed were the tomato plants, lined up neatly and bursting with bright red tomatoes. Beyond those were the cucumber plants, the jalapeño and bell peppers, and the carrots. Along the sides of the yard were a couple of tall pots, holding snapdragons, hyacinths, and bluebells. The damp and musty air smelled like an Italian restaurant.

In this certain area, I could be alone with my own thoughts to ponder on what I knew. I walked around every single bed, going over the facts I'd uncovered.

"Both the wedding and the German festival are supposed to take place on June 21st, which is a Saturday. This Saturday, to be exact. Since the German Festival is taking up all three ballrooms, this wedding isn't actually gonna happen. Since Botanica Flowers is closed on Fridays, we can't have them on time for the wedding." I fell silent and stroked a corn leaf.

"But why would Kathy do all this?" I continued. "If she actually works for the company she claims she does, the company would need to know every detail for documentation purposes. She's either just plain evil, or..." I couldn't finish my sentence. Why Kathy even did what she did was baffling me. Who was she, really?

Chapter 21
Hanaan

ver since the day that Ameerah had come over with her
d The Guy, I found myself in immense conflict about the
ea that something was wrong with Kathy and the wedding
. Ameerah's face kept forcing itself into my mind, her
ging in my ears. I couldn't stop thinking about our con-
. If anything, her revelations had only served to confirm
cions, but was that a good thing or a bad thing?

had been so upset that Rahima was getting married that
er considered what I felt about the wedding itself. It was
I didn't want the wedding to happen, but since it was
fixed event, was I okay with the event itself turning out
s?

inally, one calm afternoon when my parents were busy
rs and Rahima was occupied with something in her room,
nto my mom's laptop, searching up Tres Belle Hotel in
ser. I entered the date June 21st in the booking section,
enough, Ameerah had been right. Big bold letters saying,
for German Festival" popped up right at the top of the

Ameerah was right, I thought, creating a new tab and
"Botanica Flowers hours." I held my breath for the half
took for the search results to appear on the screen.
tanica Flowers is open every day of the week, except for Friday.
reservations now!

reathed out slowly. I had already known this, but seeing

Lost in my confusion, I walked back into the house. I was going to do more research, if that was all it took. I didn't like the idea of this wedding. I was tired of it. But Abdel-Hakeem was still my older brother, and despite the changes his decisions were making to my life, I couldn't let anything—or anyone—ruin his special day.

I hurried upstairs. I needed to use a computer, but I wasn't allowed to use Ahmed's (and who would want to anyway, considering the fact that he never cleaned it), and I couldn't raise any suspicions in Ali. Besides, he was napping right now. My last resort was Abdel–Hakeem's computer. His room was next to mine, yet separated by the staircase and held back by the railing. I turned left from the staircase and knocked on the shiny wooden door.

"Yeah?" Abdel-Hakeem asked.

"Ameerah," I said.

I heard the creaking of weight being distributed on a mattress, and then the door opened. Abdel-Hakeem stood in front of me, his hair a rumpled mess and his white shirt wrinkled where he had just been lying down. "Yo, Ameerah," he said. "What's up?"
I mentally rehearsed my prepared dialogue. This was the first time in a long time I had actually "requested" to talk to him. Clearing my throat, I said, "If it's alright, I'd like to use your computer."

My brother raised a thick eyebrow. "Oh? How come?"

"Mama told me to start looking up homeschooling curriculums." I recited another line of dialogue from my artificial script. It wasn't a lie because she had actually told me that last week, and I had put it off since then. Until now, I guess.

Abdel-Hakeem shrugged. "Alright, then, by all means, go

ahead," he said, opening the door wider. He stepped aside to let me in.

I strode inside, worry creeping over me as I remembered that Abdel-Hakeem's desk and computer both faced his bed. Anything on the screen, Abdel-Hakeem would see if he just looked my way. And with him sitting on his bed, phone in hands, there was no way he couldn't secretly spy on me.

This was not planned. But I'll figure it out. Reluctantly, I sat down at the computer. I couldn't back out now. A feeling of self-consciousness crept over me as I opened a web browser. I typed in "homeschooling curriculums" just for cover, if Abdel-Hakeem did happen to look over my shoulder unexpectedly. I hastened to find a reliable page, and after a furtive glance over my shoulder at my brother, I opened a new tab and typed "Kathy Kramer wedding planner." As I scrolled down the page, I saw a lot of Facebook and Twitter pages, but none related to a wedding company of any sort. My brow furrowed, I went back to the search engine and erased "wedding planner." Now, with just Kathy's name in the search engine, I found a lot more reliable results. Facebook pages, Twitter account, student directory...

Aha! There it was. The tiny icon that represented the college Abdel-Hakeem had attended and graduated from. I clicked on it and scrolled down the page, skimming through the writing, until I got to a page which showed photos of graduated students, then current students.

My mouth dropped open, and I struggled to keep back a gasp to avoid raising suspicion in my brother, who sat unknowingly behind me. Quickly, I closed all my tabs, cleared my history, and

closed the browser. "Uh, thanks, Abdel-I struggling to get my legs out of the swive

"Found one?" my brother asked

"One what?" I asked, completely

"Homeschool curriculum? I thin looking for."

"Oh. Right. Yeah." I gave him a "Nah, results weren't really helpful. I, ul for help." I shot for the door. "Gotta rus curriculums better than Mama, y'know, could respond, I closed his door and ma heart thumping wildly against my chest I had just seen.

"Okay," I breathed heavily, wall room. "Kathy Kramer is no one but a at that company called Her Ladyship's she used to, but was *fired* from it! Lemm stopped pacing and seized my scalp. "A But who do I tell? Abdel-Hakeem? Ma

I headed for my bed and floppe son I could tell was Hanaan! But how would she do about it? What would we

I grabbed one of my pillows ar the first time in my life, I didn't know

it right in front of me in bold print was shocking. How could this actually be happening right now? Before my own sister's wedding? After all the conflicting emotions I'd had over Rahima getting married, this was the last thing I needed on top of it all.

I didn't want my sister to get married. I didn't want her to move to a new home. But did that mean I wanted her special day to be ruined? I had seen how her eyes were shining with excitement every day. Did I want that excitement to diminish, that light to flicker out?

But then I thought about how unenthusiastic my attitude had been over the past few weeks about all and any wedding talk. What would Rahima and my parents think if I suddenly expressed concerns about the planning? Would they think I was just being a spoilsport?

I knew that I would not have been able to handle it if they brushed my suspicions aside as farfetched. *I need to gather more conclusive evidence. I need to really prove that Kathy's a fraud.*

And even though I had been upset about the wedding for so long now, I began to feel a bit excited. I was on a mission.

I firmly straightened up on my desk chair and leaned in closer to the laptop. After briefly stretching my fingers, I typed in "Kathy Kramer" in my search bar. The first few search results didn't seem very helpful so I slowly scrolled down the page.

Hmm...Aha! Student directory. Finding something that looked promising, I moved my mouse and hovered over the link to click on it. At that moment, there was a sharp tap on my door and it whirled open. Thinking fast, I immediately closed the browser and turned around to find Rahima eyeing me strangely. My heart pounded in my chest. *Did she see what I was looking at on the computer?*

But she was looking curiously at the empty spot on the wall next to my mirror. "What happened to your hadith frame?" she asked.

"Oh umm…" I was both relieved and ashamed that I had to tell her what had happened. "It broke."

"Oh my goodness, when did this happen?" She strode over to the small table where the frame had fallen, the shards of glass scattered on top.

"A few days ago," I replied as nonchalantly as possible.

"Why didn't you tell me?" Rahima held up a long shard of glass gently in her hand.

"I guess you were busy with wedding stuff," I said. Rahima looked up in surprise, and I felt a bit taken aback by my own words, too. I hadn't expected my voice to sound so bitter.

"Well, umm…" Rahima returned the piece of glass to the table. "Mama wants to order an outfit for you to wear for the wedding, so can you bring her laptop downstairs?"

I felt a bit disappointed that I wouldn't be able to continue my research about Kathy, but I nodded and stood up to follow Rahima downstairs.

"You go ahead," she said, remaining where she was standing. "I'm going to clean this glass up. I don't know how you could just keep it here, Hanaan."

I wasn't interested in hearing her lecture me about the dangers of broken glass, so I headed out of the room without another word.

My mom gave a little squeal of excitement when I entered

the living room where she was sprawled on the sofa, leaning on the arm rest. She immediately slid her legs down and reached for her laptop as she exclaimed, "Let's buy our wedding outfits, Hanaan! What color are you thinking? What style do you prefer?"

Since I hadn't actually thought about a wedding outfit until this moment, I didn't really know what to say. "I don't know. What should I get?"

"Come on, Hanaan. You always know exactly what you want to wear." It was true that I generally had a pretty good idea of how I wanted to dress on formal occasions, but this was taking me completely by surprise. What was I supposed to wear at my sister's wedding?

My mom quickly typed something and opened up a website full of an array of dazzling dresses. "Here."

She handed me the laptop, and I was momentarily stunned at the sight of all that glamor. All thoughts of the mysterious Kathy vanished.

"I can choose any of these?"

My mom chuckled. "It's your sister's wedding. We all have to look our best. And it gives us a bit of an excuse to splurge a little." She winked at me and moved in closer so she could see the page better.

I slowly scrolled down the page, passing by a swirl of colors and styles, each dress more fabulous than the last. There was glitter and sequins and all possible shades of my favorite colors. I was overwhelmed with all the choices and for once, I didn't know what to get.

Finally, I came across a breathtaking teal gown with a

delightful pattern of silver jewels on the neckline and smooth, silky pleats that I could just imagine swishing around my legs. With my sparkly silver high-heeled shoes, I would be able to make a perfect outfit. Maybe the wedding wasn't such a bad idea after all.

"This dress is perfect," my mom agreed when I showed it to her. "And Kathy was saying that it would be really nice if you walked in with the flower bouquet before the bride comes in. What do you say?"

And then, just like that, thoughts of the earlier mystery resurfaced my mind.

"Walk in with the flowers?" The excitement of getting a new dress felt somewhat tasteless now.

"Mmhmm."

"Mama," I said slowly, evading her question. "Does Kathy work as a wedding planner?"

My mom looked a little startled by the question. "What do you mean?"

"Like, is that her job?"

"Well, she doesn't work full-time, but yes, it is her job."

"So she works part-time?"

"Yeah, she's still a student at Rahima's university, so I think she works out of Her Ladyship's Day for a little extra pocket money."

"Her Ladyship's Day?"

"It's an affordable wedding planning company and it hires a lot of college students. Why so many questions?" My mom looked at me quizzically.

"Well, I just noticed that Kathy looked really young," I

sputtered. I couldn't figure out why I wasn't saying anything else.

"Okay, then, I'm going to get my credit card so we can order this dress right now." And my mom left me alone in the living room with my thoughts and one extra lead. I was going to search up Her Ladyship's Day and figure out this thing once and for all.

Chapter 22
Ameerah

It felt like forever since Ali and I had last talked. Earlier, I had watched him exhaustedly walk into the house and trudge up the stairs, which had become his habit over the three weeks he'd been working so far. I wanted to follow him, but something inside me held me back. Telling me to give him his space. But I couldn't bear to let him be. Without him, I felt lost. Alone. Yes, I had learned to entertain myself, but I missed his presence. He made everything better.

That's it. I wasn't going to deal with this distance between us anymore. I leaped off the couch where I had been watching cooking videos on Mama's laptop and thumped up the stairs two by two.

"Ali?" I called out once I reached the top of the stairs. His open door indicated that Ahmed wasn't in. I crossed the wooden floorboards to reach the room and peeked inside. I hoped Ali was awake. It had been two hours since he came home, and he usually woke up around now. I just hoped he would be up for a conversation with me.

Sure enough, there he was on his side of the room. But this time, he wasn't using his computer or his phone, or even his bed. He was jogging on his treadmill with his earbuds locked in.

I stood at the door for a while, enthralled. He hadn't used his treadmill in ages. Seeing him working out and sticking to his usual hobbies ignited a little candle inside me. It made me happy. It reminded me of the old Ali. The Ali I used to know. The Ali who would tell me everything, listen to all my stories, offer needed advice, protect me no matter what the costs, and spend time with me. I missed that Ali. I needed him back.

I tapped my signature knock on the door, louder than usual. *Tap-taptaptap.*

At first, my brother didn't hear the knock, and I didn't expect him to because he was listening to his nasheeds. So I knocked again, and this time I took one step into the room. "Ali," I said loudly.

My brother glanced my way, and once he spotted me, he immediately turned off his treadmill and pulled out his earbuds. Breathing too heavily to speak, he beckoned me over.

"Hi," I said eagerly once I reached him. "Do you need water or anything?"

Ali sank down on his bed. Beads of sweat covered his forehead. "I could use some, yeah," he panted. "Do you mind—"

"On it." I sprang up from the bed and hurried downstairs to fill a glass with water, then tried not to spill it as I ran back upstairs to Ali's room.

"Thanks, princess," Ali said with a smile.

The fact that he had called me by my nickname poured guilt all over me. When someone called me princess, it meant they were in a good mood or they were trying to make me feel better. But I was about to lash out at Ali. My favorite brother. Whatever I said to him was going to ruin this moment. But I had to do it. I was not going to allow this distance between us any longer. I handed my brother the glass and sat beside him as he took large gulps.

"So," I began, gripping the mattress with both hands,

"you've been pretty busy at work, huh?"

Ali glanced at me, lowered the glass from his mouth, and said, "Yeah. Pretty much." He shot a quizzical look at me, indicating I say more.

I looked away and swung my legs, carefully picking out my words. "It's important, isn't it?"

"Yeah..."

"More important than me?" The bitter words escaped my mouth before I could stop them.

Ali switched from a side glance to turning his full face towards me. "What?"

I struggled to keep my voice steady. "Ever since you started work, you haven't been able to spend time with me. I wanted to spend the summer hanging out with you, but now I can't because your job takes up the entire summer!"

"Well—" Ali began.

"And why didn't you tell me about this job? I was the last one to know about it. Don't you always make sure I'm the first one to know about everything?"

Ali placed the glass between his feet and touched my shoulder. "Ameerah, calm down. Listen. I would have told you, okay? I was going to tell you the day I applied for the job. But on that day, you weren't around because you were out practicing for your big game. Then my boss started calling me and asking me to schedule an interview, and I had to write up my resume to show him, and all of that kinda stuff. He kept texting me about a bunch of stuff I would need to know before I started the job, making sure that this job was something I was gonna be happy with. Anyway, I

eventually forgot to tell you with everything going on, and then, on the day of your game, which I couldn't go to because of the event at the masjid, I remembered I had to tell you. Then when I got that text at dinner and you asked a bunch of questions, I realized I still hadn't told you, and I felt bad. I felt guilty. I really did. So... I'm sorry, Ameerah. I wanted to tell you, trust me. And I wanted to apologize, but I just didn't know how. Or when. I didn't know how you'd take it."

The story silenced me. I felt guilty. Ali really wanted the best for me. Anything he did or didn't do wasn't intended to hurt me in any way. I suppressed the tears I'd been wanting to let out and sniffed.

"Well, I guess now you know, huh?" I looked up at my brother with a tiny smirk.

Ali laughed. "Yeah, I do. So," he wrapped his arm around my shoulders, "do you forgive me?"

Those words alone did it. My heart fluttered with happiness, bringing a big grin to my face. Brimming with joy, I threw my arms around my big brother in a hug. "I love you, Ali."

My brother chuckled and squeezed me back. "I love you back, Meera. And I still have time to spend with you on weekends, okay? You just need to push me a little more."

"Yeah, I know how you love your sleep," I grinned. "You sleep like a baby."

"Hey, I'm sixteen, but I'm still growing!"

"So you say. Okay, you can let go of me now."

Ali released me, and we sat together in silence for a moment. My gaze darted around the room, locking on the iPad and laptop on Ali's desk. Seeing them sparked the question I had been wanting to ask him for so long. "Hey, what do you even do at work?"

Ali shrugged. "Oh, I make posters, flyers, business cards, brochures, basically anything else you can do with graphic art. At the building, we work in a warehouse, carrying around heavy boxes of random things. The graphic art stuff is kind of my homework."

"So why are you always on your phone?" I asked.

Ali counted off on his fingers. "My boss texts me information for the flyers, the agenda for the upcoming work day, changes and updates to the warehouse, and whether or not he needs to send his assistant to direct us."

"He tells you all these things twenty-four seven?" I asked, raising my eyebrows knowingly.

"Well, sure, you could say that." Ali bent down to pick up his glass and took another big gulp.

"Come on, Ali. Even your boss has to have a life outside of his phone."

Ali almost snorted and quickly placed the glass back on the floor. "Okay, okay," he laughed. "My friends text me too."

I grinned. "Mm-hmm. Go on."

My brother shook his head at me. "Also, we host community events. In fact, we have one coming up this Saturday." He shrugged. "A German festival, they said."

German festival. Aha! "Oh, hey, speaking of which," I said casually, "in terms of your job, remember when I came in here a few days ago, and you shooed me out?"

Ali looked a little guilty. "Oh, sorry about that. It took me so long to make the flyer because my first version didn't save and I had to redo it all over again. That's why I was worried when I saw you using my computer."

Oh. That explains it, I thought. But I wasn't to be sidetracked. "I saw the flyer."

Ali took a sip of water. "What did you think?"

"Well, I *thought* Abdel-Hakeem was supposed to have his wedding in the Tres Belle Hotel," I replied, giving him my dramatic look in hopes that it would bring him back to his senses.

"Wait, what?" Ali was confused. "What does his wedding have to do with my flyer?"

He's not getting it! I intensified the tone of my voice. "If I remember correctly, *your flyer* said the *German festival* is at the *Tres Belle Hotel.* The *same* place the *wedding* is supposed to be! On the same *day!*"

Ali's eyes grew wide. "Oh no. Really?" He snatched his iPad off his computer table and opened the flyer. "Tres Belle Hotel. That's where he's having the wedding? Really?"

"Yeah!" I said, heaving a big sigh. *Finally!* "I thought you'd have known that, but I guess your work made you forget about everything else."

"Are you sure?" Ali was now swiftly swiping through his phone, scouring text messages with whom I guessed was his infamous boss. "Maybe I got the wrong date," he muttered. His swiping slowed on a certain cluster of messages. "No, it is the 21st! Oh, no. They explicitly said the festival would be taking up the entire rentable facility. Abdel-Hakeem would have known that!"

"Yeah, well..." I curled my toes in the carpet. "He hasn't

been planning this by himself. He's got a wedding planner handling everything. And because of that, his wedding is going to be a total blow and Kathy Kramer is gonna take his money!"

Both of Ali's thick eyebrows furrowed, like two hairy brown caterpillars asking me what the heck I was babbling about. "What, Ameerah? A total blow? Who's Kathy?"

I told him everything I had discovered about the wedding plans and Kathy's intention to steal Abdel-Hakeem's money.

"And like you have just realized," I finished, "that German festival you made a flyer for is going to be taking up all the ball-rooms, and Kathy said she reserved just one for us. She's lying, see?"

"Yes, I see!" Ali exclaimed. "Ameerah, why didn't you tell Abdel-Hakeem? The wedding is supposed to happen in two days and if you don't say anything now, it won't happen at all! You gotta tell him!"

"I didn't tell him because—"

Ali cut me off. "Excuses later! C'mon, let's tell him now!" He motioned for me to get off his bed.

I leaped up and sprinted across the hall to Abdel-Hakeem's room. *Bang bang bang!*

"It's me, Ameerah!" I called through the wood, and in seconds, Ali was behind me.

Immediately, my eldest brother opened the door. "Yo, what's all the fuss?" he asked. "What's up with you two?"

"Let us in!" I said. "We'll tell you."

Bewildered, Abdel-Hakeem stepped aside and opened the door wider. "Man," he said after we had walked in. "I haven't been on high demand this much in years!"

"Sorry, Abdel-Hakeem, but what I have to say is no joke," I said. "Sit down and listen."

Abdel-Hakeem shot Ali a look, but Ali just shrugged and tipped his chin at me. We all sat down on Abdel-Hakeem's bed, Ali and I sitting on each side of our big brother. I let out a big breath. "Okay, I'm just gonna say it straight out," I began. "Your wedding is gonna be a blow."

"Say what?" My eldest brother had a small smirk on his face.

Ugh. He doesn't believe me. I pressed on. "Your wedding planner, Kathy Kramer, is a total fake. She's been lying to you about everything. She said she would get the flowers for you on Friday, right? Botanica flowers? Well, get this. Botanica is closed on Fridays."

Abdel-Hakeem held up a hand, trying to edge in a word, but I swatted it away. "And what was that you said this morning? That she reserved a ballroom for you guys? Not happening! Apparently, the Tres Belle hotel has booked events all month, and your wedding isn't one of them. Do you know what event is taking up all three ballrooms instead? A German festival. Isn't that right, Ali?" I nodded my chin at him.

"Yeah," Ali confirmed. "I made a flyer for it."

"What's more," I went on, "Kathy doesn't work for that company she claims she does. In fact, she was fired from it!"

Abdel-Hakeem stared incredulously first at me, then at Ali, then at me again. He was silent for a moment, and then he began to smirk. "C'mon, Ameerah! How badly do you not want me to get married, huh?"

Behind him, Ali rolled his eyes.

"I'm not gonna fall for that," my eldest brother continued.

"Abdel-Hakeem, it's the truth!" I insisted. "And if we don't do something about it right now, your wedding is not going to happen at all!"

With a chuckle, my eldest brother glanced at Ali and raised his eyebrow. "So exactly how many tries did it take for y'all to practice this little act here?"

"Abdel-Hakeem, she's serious," Ali said. "Ameerah wouldn't joke about something like this."

"Ugh! Just give me your phone!" I huffed impatiently.

Abdel-Hakeem slid his phone out of his pocket and handed it over. Swiftly, I opened Google Chrome and pulled up the website for the Tres Belle Hotel. "Look," I said, showing my brother the calendar. "Booked here, here, everywhere! The whole month."

Abdel-Hakeem's eyes darted over the phone screen. "Well," he said finally, clearing his throat, "this is certainly weird." Anxiously, he smoothed his hair out of his face.

"Yeah, so what are you gonna do?" I asked, handing his phone back.

Shaking his head, Abdel-Hakeem took the phone and opened the number pad. "God, I dunno. I gotta talk to Rahima."

Chapter 23
Hanaan

"Hanaan?" The curtain behind me fluttered and Rahima's voice startled me out of my thoughts. "Can I join you?"

Surprised, I moved over and patted the hard rooftop beside me. Rahima had never come out to Fajr's Shadow with me before, but she climbed out of my window with surprising ease and skill. As she took a seat beside me, I caught a glimpse of a wrinkled piece of paper folded in her hand.

"Wow, it is pretty nice out here," she remarked, gazing out into the neighborhood.

"That's what I've been telling you."

"It's kind of uncomfortable, though. Too hard to sit on." She adjusted her sitting position.

"I guess I'm just used to it," I said.

"Hmm…" Rahima looked out dreamily at the expanse of houses and trees that lined the street.

"I was strolling around the backyard earlier," she said suddenly, still looking ahead of her.

"Oh?"

"I was just thinking about how much I'm going to miss living in this house. I don't think I've ever really appreciated how beautiful our neighborhood is."

I didn't say anything. This was the first time I had heard her really talking about her moving out, and I wasn't sure if I wanted to hear her talk about it.

"I noticed many interesting things back there," Rahima

continued, still not looking at me.

"Oh?" I didn't know why she was telling me this, but as long as I didn't have to say anything…

"You remember that little tree we planted there back when you were five?"

I nodded. I still checked it out regularly to see it progress through the seasons.

"It's grown so tall in the past few years."

I rubbed my finger against the wood absentmindedly as Rahima kept talking.

"And remember that time we tried to mimic a cannon and shoot water balloons into the front yard? And then we tried it out with a heavy rock and smashed a hole through the fence?"

I smiled at the memory and nodded, thinking about the misshapen hole at an awkward angle in the fence.

"The hole is still there! I can't believe I haven't thought about that day in so long. Remember Mama was furious that we had been playing with the heavy rock? But Baba was laughing so hard!"

"Yeah."

"You know what else I noticed in the backyard? Remember that day we found a dead bird on the back deck and you were so sad? And then we buried it in the corner of the lawn and marked the spot with a stick?"

I nodded again. I still noticed it every now and then when I went into the backyard, but hearing Rahima talk about it reminded me that all these were symbols of our shared childhood memories together.

"You always felt things a lot more keenly than I did," Rahima mused. "Like I was sad about the bird, too, but you? You were literally crying because you kept thinking about the bird's family. I hadn't even thought that the bird might have a family, but you imagined the bird's whole family and life out."

And I still remembered the bird's life story, all the way up to how he died and ended up in our backyard.

"I found one more thing out in the backyard." This time, Rahima didn't elaborate. She wordlessly unfolded the piece of paper that was tucked in her hand and passed it to me. Confused, I spread out the paper in front of me and then gaped at it when I realized what it was. The words were written in my own handwriting. This paper was the one I had written on this very same spot over a week ago.

I read through my words again, my heart brimming with emotion.

BETRAYAL

Two beloved sisters,
Like brownies to ice cream
Butter to bread
And honey to the comb.

We shared with each other
Every single thought and emotion
Every secret, every whisper
Just between me and my only sister.

The Summer When Everything Changed

When I was upset,
I knew who to look for.
Who would comfort and cajole me
And hug me all the more.

And about her, I knew
All that went through
All her secrets and stories
All her memories and jokes

I'm here, she said
A comfort I am for you and you are for me,
And happy together
We always will be

Then I opened up my heart,
But she broke it apart
I'm here, said she
But then I lost her with time

An unwelcome hand
Disrupted our joy
He said he loved her
But I saw him as a decoy.

How did I feel then?
She bombarded me with pain
With deception and deceit

It was nothing but insane.
She left everything
Our sisterhood and friendship
She forgot it all
Without a thought of me

Did she know what she was doing?
Did she know I was affected?
Was I ever on her mind?
Was I a victim of betrayal?

Because that's how I felt.
The heartbreak, the loneliness.
The tears and the fury.
That felt like betrayal.

Rahima was still staring straight ahead, apparently focusing very hard at some strangely shaped clouds. "Remember when I was in twelfth grade? And I was going to go on that week-long trip with some other high school seniors to visit a few colleges around the east coast?"

Instead of waiting for me to respond, she continued talking. "You were so upset that I was going to be gone for a week and you kept saying how much you were going to miss me and how much you didn't want me to go. You were just so sad and it made me feel so bad later because I realized that I had been talking so much about how excited I was for the trip that I hadn't considered how it was affecting you."

I remembered this trip very clearly and how it had been

canceled at the last minute because a bus had broken down. It had been a very anticlimactic end to all the previous anticipation on Rahima's part and dread on my end.

"When I didn't end up going on the trip, I thought about how all those weeks that you were upset that I was going had all really been a waste."

I didn't know why Rahima was talking about this, but I had a feeling I was about to find out.

"When I started to talk to Abdel-Hakeem seriously, like about marriage, my first instinct was to tell you all about it. But then I stopped to think for once and remembered how hard you took it when I was going to go on that trip for just a week. And I thought about how much harder if would be for you if I said I might get married and move out. So then I thought, if this doesn't work out and I don't end up marrying Abdel-Hakeem, was it really worth it to tell you about it? So I decided to wait."

"I'm not eight anymore, Heema," I said quietly.

"I know," Rahima replied. She slipped her arm around me, pulling me close. "Maybe I should've given you more credit. But I didn't want to see you upset. Not unnecessarily. Don't you understand?"

I didn't reply, but I moved in closer and lay my head on her shoulder.

"You can't imagine how much I love you, Hanaan. My little sister."

Leaning in close to my sister, just the two of us in my most special place, I breathed in the moment, not wanting it to end. But try as I might, I could not get rid of the nagging sensation in my

mind. Here was Rahima, holding me close, telling me she only wanted the best for me. And me? I was spitefully keeping a secret that could end up turning very hurtful for her.

The wedding was in two days. There was still lots of time for everything to mess up, but by the time everyone else realized it, it was going to be too late. It was probably too late already. I mean, how much can one fix in less than forty-eight hours?

"Rahima," I said slowly, forcing myself to speak.

"Hmm?"

"I have to tell you something, okay?"

Rahima noted the serious tone my voice had taken, and she said, "Okay."

"You're probably going to be mad, and I don't know why I've been keeping this a secret, but I think you should know. I mean, you have to know because it's about you."

"Hanaan." Rahima turned her gaze to me and furrowed her eyebrows. "What are you trying to say?"

I straightened up, took a deep breath and avoided Rahima's gaze as I blurted out, "Kathy is a fraud, she's been lying about everything, and your wedding is going to be ruined."

She looked a bit shocked. "What?"

"Please don't say you don't believe me, okay? At first I thought it was just me, but Ameerah noticed that she was suspicious, too, and…"

"Ameerah? You've talked about this with Ameerah?" It seemed that this was more unbelievable than my accusations towards Kathy.

"Well, yeah. Ameerah was the one who figured out that the

hotel place was reserved for a German festival, and when I told her about the flowers…"

"What do you mean 'reserved for a German festival'?" Rahima was making me nervous every time she interrupted me.

"Just listen, okay? Kathy isn't really employed by that wedding planning company. I checked the website and her name isn't anywhere on there. And it's not just because she's a college student; there are loads of other college students on there. And I checked out her social media pages, and, well, I think she was fired from the company a little while ago."

"Is that so?" I couldn't read Rahima's expression, so I kept talking.

"And the Tres Belle hotel? It's reserved for other events all month, and there's a big German festival on June 21st. And Botanica Flowers is closed on Fridays so basically everything she's promised to do is really just a lie."

"Hanaan, how long have you known this?"

I squirmed a bit. "Well, umm, I only found out all the details yesterday, but I started getting suspicious when Ameerah came over the other day when Kathy was here."

"That was Sunday, Hanaan. You've known this since Sunday?"

"That's when I just started to figure out that Kathy wasn't all she said she was. I didn't know enough to actually accuse of her anything."

"Well, were you planning on telling me any of this before Saturday?"

"Umm, yeah, I just couldn't find the right moment."

"The right moment? The right moment, Hanaan? The wedding is in two days. It's the day after tomorrow."

"I know, but…" I was interrupted by a sudden vibrating. I gasped loudly and almost slipped out of surprise. I grasped in the air for something to hold onto and heard Rahima squeal as she held onto me tightly.

"Wait, wait, it's my phone," Rahima said sheepishly, reaching into her pocket to retrieve the source of the vibration. I glanced at the screen and saw Abdel-Hakeem's name on top. My heart started beating a million times a minute, and I tried to think of a way to distract Rahima, but the next moment she was accepting the call.

"Hello?"

"Assalamu alaikum, Rahima," I heard Abdel-Hakeem say a bit anxiously.

Ameerah must have told him, I realized, suddenly grateful that I had been able to tell Rahima about it before Ameerah got to her brother.

"Wa alaikumussalam," Rahima was saying on the phone.

"Where are you?"

"I'm on the roof."

"Okay, we need to…wait, what?"

"Never mind. We need to what?"

"We need to talk about the wedding."

"Why? Are you having second thoughts?" Rahima teased. I shook my head at her. How could she be joking around right now?

"No. Are you?" I couldn't believe it. Were neither of them taking this seriously?

I nudged my sister. *"Heema?!"* I could've sworn I heard a similar fierce whisper on the other end of the phone line saying, "Abdel-Hakeem!"

"Alright, alright," Rahima conceded. "We have to meet up right away and sort this thing out."

"Are you talking about this Kathy person?"

"Yes, I am talking about this Kathy person. Hanaan was just telling me about her fabulous findings. She basically stalked Kathy everywhere on the Internet and probably knows all her student and job history, not to mention maybe a couple of dogs she once owned."

"I did not stalk her!" I protested, but Rahima seemed to be enjoying herself. Did she not realize that all her wedding plans were literally nonexistent and that there was no time to waste?

"Ameerah's been busy looking Kathy up, too," I heard Abdel-Hakeem say through the phone. "I don't know, but for someone who's acted so uninterested in this whole wedding prep thing, she sure has done a lot of research about it." This time, I could hear Ameerah muttering something in the background.

"It is very touching that our sisters have invested their time for looking into this," Rahima agreed. "Perhaps it would have been a bit more helpful for them to mention it a bit sooner, but I guess better late than never, huh, Hanaan?"

I didn't say anything.

"Well," Abdel-Hakeem said. "It's not the wedding day yet."

"Yup, we have a whole forty-eight hours left," Rahima said. Looking down at her watch, she corrected herself, "Actually a bit less than that. I'm going to call Kathy now, okay? Let's see what she has to say for herself.”

“Alright, then y’all come over so we can talk about this in person and figure out what to do next.”

“Okay. Assalamu alaikum.” Rahima ended the phone call and snapped her phone case shut. “Alright, let’s do this thing,” she said, turning to me. Then, she looked back at the window behind her. “Do I have to go through that thing again?”

“Want a push?” I suggested, grinning a bit maliciously.

“No way, you cheeky monkey!” She carefully turned around, climbed up on her hands and knees and made her way through the window back into my room. The sight of her crawling on the roof like that was too much for me. I was laughing as I followed her through the window.

Everything had turned upside down. The wedding was probably all ruined and now, we were on the way to Ameerah’s house. But for the first time in weeks, I felt light-hearted inside. My relationship with Rahima was the same as it had always been, and I knew that no matter what happened next, she would always be my special sister.

Chapter 24
Ameerah

"What do you mean we don't have a wedding hall?!"
I winced as my mother's voice resounded through the house. From my place in the living room, I could hear Abdel-Hakeem murmuring something in response. I strained my ears to hear what he was saying, but the next moment my effort was unnecessary because my mom's voice had increased in volume.

"Don't tell me to calm down, Abdel-Hakeem Salleh! We have two hundred people coming for this thing and…"

A door closed, and her voice was suddenly muffled. I began to consider whether to abandon my post in the living room and go upstairs to hear the conversation better when the doorbell rang. I immediately jumped up from the sofa, ran across the room in two strides and pulled the front door open.

Rahima and her mother murmured their salams to me and stepped into the house. For a moment, I thought they had left Hanaan behind, but I saw her follow the other two a bit sheepishly. I stood there, refusing to meet their gazes, as I watched them remove their shoes.

"Ameerah," Rahima said in a soft voice. I unintentionally caught her eye and was surprised to see a twinkle lurking in there. "Can you let Abdel-Hakeem know that we're here?"

"Yeah, I'll be right back." I skipped off towards the stairs, then realized I hadn't invited them in and quickly retraced my steps. "You can sit in the living room," I added, motioning for them to sit down.

Aunty Nusaybah came in and seated herself on the sofa, a very serious expression on her face. Hanaan followed close behind. And Rahima, for a second it looked as if she was holding back a grin. But of course I was just imagining things, I told myself. Rahima must have been furious about everything that was going on.

A few minutes later, everyone was gathered together in the living room having an intense conversation. Both mothers were alternately discussing options and scolding Rahima and Abdel-Hakeem for letting things get out of hand. The soon-to-be groom and bride seemed concerned but unrattled and mostly seemed determined to calm the mothers down. Hanaan was sitting inches away from me, but she hadn't said a word to me yet. Even I didn't want to say anything or draw any attention to myself, but I tried to catch Hanaan's eye and get a sense of how she was feeling.

I had been paying so much attention to Hanaan that I didn't realize right away that a heated conversation was already in full swing.

"This is absolutely ridiculous," my mother was saying. "We need to get a hold of this woman and make sure she doesn't get away with this."

"But isn't the wedding the priority right now?" Hanaan's mother responded. She shot a stern look in Rahima's direction and sharpened her tone. "We need to figure out how to clean up this disaster these two have put us in."

Rahima turned to her mother with a convincing aura of confidence about herself. "I know this is all really overwhelming, especially with the wedding this weekend, but Abdel-Hakeem and I can handle this."

"Yeah, that's what you said before all this happened! How do you plan on fixing this?"

Abdel-Hakeem spoke up. "We contacted Miss Kramer, and she should be here any moment. When she comes, we will confront her about the concerns we had, and depending on her response, we will make our next move, insha Allah."

As soon as the words left his lips, the doorbell rang. At first, no one moved or spoke. Then, Mama broke the silence. "You better hope she has a good explanation for everything," she said in a fierce whisper.

Abdel-Hakeem made a move towards the door and Rahima and the moms stood up, as well. But before they had taken so much as two steps, Mama turned to me and sternly said, "Ameerah, out. Take Hanaan to your room, and don't come down until I call you."

What? Leave the meeting? "But Mama!" I protested. "Why can't I stay?"

"I don't want to hear another word. Out, I said."

There was no way I was going to miss out on this meeting! I looked to the others for help, but Hanaan's mom was nudging her to leave, too. Rahima was just smiling sympathetically and Abdel-Hakeem didn't even look in our direction. Grumpily, I gave in and headed toward the stairs, but tried to walk as slowly as possible in case I could catch any of the conversation. Hanaan seemed to have the same thing in mind since she was taking tiny steps toward me. Silently, sullenly, we made our way up the winding staircase. "It's not fair," I muttered once we reached my room, out of earshot of the adults.

"I know," Hanaan replied in a surprisingly calm voice. "But

it's not really fair that Rahima and… your brother's wedding is ruined either."

"Yeah, but like they wouldn't even have known about Kathy's lies if it weren't for us. And now they're making us miss the confrontation. We deserve to be there!"

"I would like to see Kathy speechless for once," Hanaan said thoughtfully. "What do you think she's gonna say when she realizes Abdel-Hakeem and Rahima know the truth?"

"I wish I could see her face when she finds out," I grumbled.

"Maybe we can't exactly see her face, but…" Hanaan hesitated.

"But what?"

"Nothing, except, well, maybe we could hear some of it if we stood at the top of the stairs or something." Her face reddened slightly, and she seemed to almost regret her words.

"Wow, Hanaan, you shock me," I said teasingly. "I didn't know you were a rebel."

"I'm not!" Hanaan protested, her face getting even redder. "You were the one complaining that you couldn't hear what they're talking about."

I grinned and stood up, suddenly getting an idea. "We won't hear them from the top of the stairs, but I know where we can if they are sitting in the dining room."

I indicated for her to follow me and led her to the end of the hallway where I knelt down and pressed my ear against an air vent on the floor.

"Um, what are you doing?" Hanaan raised her eyebrows at

my awkward position.

"This air vent connects to the air vent downstairs," I explained, pulling her down beside me.

Hanaan hesitated for only a moment before pressing her ear beside mine. "I don't hear anything. Are you sure…" Muffled voices floated up, cutting Hanaan short.

"We know you've been working really hard to get everything ready for Saturday," Rahima was saying.

I snorted loudly, and Hanaan elbowed me sharply in the side. "Sorry," she apologized immediately.

"Shh," I replied.

"You're the one who's making noise!"

We shuffled a bit and by time we quieted down again, Kathy was speaking.

"I don't know what you're implying, nothing bad about Her Ladyship's Day, I hope?"

"Well, I certainly hope not," Abdel-Hakeem said.

"Look, we're not trying to point fingers at anyone," Rahima said. "We just want to get to the bottom of everything. We're not feeling very confident that all our wedding plans are in motion."

Kathy chuckled a bit nervously. "It's perfectly normal to feel bridal jitters and overreact to things right before the wedding. I don't want you to worry about all that. That's why I'm here, remember?"

"I don't want to worry about all that, either," Rahima replied, "but…"

Abdel-Hakeem cut in. "Look, here, Miss Kramer. Whatever you may be doing or not doing, don't go blaming my fiancée for anything that goes wrong. We hired you for a purpose, and it doesn't seem like you've been committing yourself to that role. Why don't you just admit it so we're all on the same page?"

"How dare you make such accusations?" Kathy was clearly riled up now. "Not only is this an insult to me personally, but this is also an attack on our company!"

"Let's not take that route, Miss Kramer," Rahima said softly. "We know you don't work for Her Ladyship's Day anymore."

"Wh-what?" Kathy's voice was very low, and I strained my ears to hear, but suddenly, Hanaan lifted her head and sat up on her knees.

"What are you doing?" I hissed at her.

"I don't know. This just feels kinda wrong. I'm not enjoying this as much as I thought I would."

I felt torn inside, but reluctantly sat up beside her. "Somehow, I'm not enjoying this either," I admitted.

"I think it's because we all secretly thought Kathy would have some sort of explanation that would make everything right," Hanaan said thoughtfully. "But I don't think she does, and now the wedding really is ruined."

Hearing Hanaan say that so bluntly rattled me more than I thought it would. We sat in silence for a few moments until we heard rapid footsteps downstairs and the front door slam. We looked at each other for a moment, then rushed to the stairs.

"How is this happening right now? What are we going to do about the wedding, the halls, the guests...about everything?" My mom's voice indicated that she was near her breaking point.

"It's not time to panic, Mama," Abdel-Hakeem said calmly.

"We'll figure this out."

"Oh, you will, will you? What do you plan on doing on Saturday morning when guests start calling?"

While Abdel-Hakeem tried to calm her down, Hanaan's mom was talking angrily on the phone. "Where are you? Your daughter's wedding is in complete ruins and you're at work? Your eldest daughter!"

Hanaan and I exchanged looks. It didn't seem like a good idea to go down right now. But the next moment, Abdel-Hakeem's voice called out my name. When I had reached the bottom step, he looked at me with a relieved expression and said, "Ameerah, can you do me a favor and get a cold drink for Mama, Aunty Nusaybah, and Rahima?"

"Don't worry about me, Ameerah," Rahima said a bit distractedly as she typed something in her phone. Suddenly, she gasped excitedly, a broad grin spreading itself across her face. I paused at the threshold of the staircase to see what was going on. Hanaan was standing close behind me, her eyes resting on her sister.

"Rahima!" Hanaan's mom scolded. "Now is not the time to fool around. Will you ever take anything seriously?"

"No, no. I mean yes! I mean...listen. It's Jamilah. She just replied...well, I mean texted."

Aunty Nusaybah glared at her, perplexed and irritated. "This is not the time to be incoherent, Rahima."

"Okay, it's like this." Rahima lifted her face, her gaze rapturous, her voice slightly trembling with excitement. "Earlier, when Hanaan first told me of her doubts about Kathy, I immediately texted Jamilah and asked her what the current status of reservations was at Masjid Nurayn. She had told me a few weeks ago that it was booked for another event on Saturday because she knew I was interested, but I told her you wanted it to be at Tres Belle Hotel instead. But right now, she just texted me that the reservation for Saturday was just canceled yesterday, and the wedding hall is completely available. And get this. The caterers for the event that was canceled are still willing to cater the food for us as long as we get the payment in by tomorrow evening. Everything is falling into place, and it's just how we wanted it to be."

The room was completely silent. No one said anything for a moment. Then, Abdel-Hakeem spoke up. "Well. Alhamdulillah for that. Let's finalize this and then start contacting all the guests to let them know about the change of venue. Ameerah, can you get those drinks?" I nodded and headed to the kitchen, Hanaan following close behind.

As I began pouring orange juice into a glass, she quietly came beside me and held out another glass. "Rahima's always wanted to get married at Masjid Nurayn, you know?" she said suddenly. "Ever since it opened, I mean."

"Really?" I thought about the masjid that had opened a few years ago that had an enormous dome structure and a magnificent courtyard. The entire facility was beautiful, and I vaguely remembered hearing Abdel-Hakeem say something about renting the event hall there, but I knew both my mom and Aunty Nusaybah had wanted to have the wedding at Tres Belle Hotel, so I hadn't thought that Rahima wanted it any different. I silently poured the remainder of the juice and returned the bottle to the fridge.

Hanaan and I each held a drink and headed back to the living room, walking slowly so the juice wouldn't spill. The animated chatter from the living room increased in volume as we approached the others. When we reached the end of the hallway, Hanaan leaned close to me and said, "Well, it looks like we are having a wedding after all, like it or not. Do you think you can handle it?"

I grinned. "I think I'm strong enough to handle it. What about you?"

"I'll take my chances."

Chapter 25
Hanaan

"It's almost 12:30. Where are you guys?"

"The last car! We're leaving!"

"Wait! You can't leave without the bride!"

"Where is the bride?"

"Rahima! The wedding can't happen without you. Where are you?"

My mom, grandma and aunts were aflutter with excitement as they rushed about to make sure everything was set to head off to the masjid. My dad and the rest of our family who were already there had left over half an hour ago. Ameerah's family and our close family friends were supposed to be there, too.

I was dressed in my new wedding outfit, standing awkwardly aside as everyone else pinned each other's clothes and added last minute touches to their outfits. I heard my mom call for Rahima, and a familiar light-hearted chuckle floated down the stairs. "We still have plenty of time, Mama. The guests aren't supposed to arrive until 1."

My great-aunt shook her head forebodingly. "She's going to be late, that one. And why is she so calm? It's making me nervous." She turned to me. "Hanaan, go up there and hurry your sister along. Remind her that all her future in-laws are waiting for her at the masjid."

I suppressed a smile at the thought of the Sallehs forming a straight line at the gate of the masjid, awaiting Rahima's arrival. As I walked up the stairs, the giggles and excited chatter from

Rahima's room became louder and louder. I paused at her door, unsure whether I wanted to see Rahima all dressed up yet. I had been at her side the whole morning, but when her friends had come over to help her get dressed, I had left, not quite ready to see her as a bride.

Summoning up my courage, I lifted my fingers and tapped gently on the door.

"We're almost ready, Aunty Nusaybah," I heard Rahima's friend Khadijah call. "Just a few more touches here and there — "

"Hush!" Rahima interrupted her. "That's not my mom. It's Hanaan." I could hear the room immediately go silent and imagined Rahima nod to Sumayyah or Hajar to open the door. Quiet footsteps crossed the length of the room, and the door opened. But when I looked up, it wasn't Sumayyah or Hajar looking at me. It wasn't even Khadijah. It was someone else. Someone dressed in a magnificent gown, her head wrapped in a shining hijab adorned with jewelry, her face glowing brightly. This remarkable personage smiled at me, and then I knew it was my sister.

"I've been waiting for you, Hanaan," she said. "So, how do I look?"

"Umm, nice," I responded a bit shyly. I had never been shy of my sister before, but seeing her decked out in this way was making me feel weird. Like she was a different person, stepping into a new role and out of her old place.

"Nice?" Sumayyah scoffed cheekily. "We've been working on your sister for hours, and all you can say is that she looks nice?"

"Hanaan's not easily impressed. Do we have to start all over again, Rahima?" Hajar teased.

"Nuh-uh, I'm through with you, girl!" Khadijah stepped back and swiped at Hajar with a stray cloth in her hand.

"Yo, watch it!" Hajar whisked the cloth out of Khadijah's hand and held it over her menacingly.

"Oh, Lord!" Sumayyah rolled her eyes. "Can y'all act a bit more mature right now? Our girl is getting married in like two hours." The two stopped their fooling around and stood up straight, as if awaiting instruction.

Rahima grinned at them. "You guys are the best. Can you go get everyone downstairs into the car and tell them that the bride is officially ready?"

"Hah, they won't believe it until they see it," Hajar pronounced.

"Aren't you coming, too, Rahima?" Khadijah asked quizzically. "You're sorta the priority right now."

"In a few minutes."

"Nostalgia," Hajar said in a loud whisper. "She wants to look around her room for the last time as a singleton."

"I think it's more like private sister-to-sister talk," Sumayyah said in a superior tone, ushering the others out of the room.

I started a bit at that statement and tried to avoid Rahima's gaze, making an attempt to leave the room, too. But Rahima closed the door behind Sumayyah, leaving the two of us alone in the room.

"Are you ready for this?" Rahima looked at me intently, searching for an answer hidden in my eyes.

"I dunno. Are you?"

Rahima laughed. "I hope so."

"Well," I said. I didn't know what else to say.

"Hanaan, I know things haven't been turning out the way you wanted them to."

"Well, things haven't been turning out that great for you either," I admitted. "Your wedding was almost ruined."

Rahima laughed again, bright as ever, and warmth flooded through me at the sound. "Honestly, I think everything has turned out for the better. You know I wanted my wedding at Masjid Nurayn all along. And you? You saved the day. You're basically the hero of my story."

"Well, it wasn't just me." I didn't want to take all the credit when I knew that I probably wouldn't have figured everything out without Ameerah.

"I know," Rahima nodded. "And I love how you and Ameerah were able to set aside your differences and carve out a special relationship of your own. You two make a great team."

I tilted my head to one side, mulling over her words. Rahima was right. Even though our relationship had been rocky at first, to say the least, Ameerah and I had created something special between us. I could tell that the two of us would come to treasure the bond we would soon have once our older siblings married each other. And considering how Rahima and Abdel-Hakeem had pulled together to solve what could have been a terrible fiasco, I knew they made a good team, too.

"I will never forget this day, Hanaan, and the role you played to make it happen. And I don't want you to ever forget that you will always have a special place in my heart, okay?"

Rahima was placing a package in my hands before I

realized what was happening.

"What's this?" I asked curiously, even though some part of me already knew what I was holding.

"Open it," Rahima said with a twinkle in her eye.

I removed the packaging and uncovered a brand new frame, similar to my previous one, yet infinitely more awe-inspiring. The fonts were darker, the colors were bolder, the glass was more shiny, and the entire thing just seemed more distinguished than my old one.

"The two lights," I murmured.

"You won't forget this time, right, Hanaan?" Rahima's eyes pierced mine, and I could feel the love emanating from within. I responded with a nod and a smile, holding my new frame tightly in my hands.

"Rahimaaa!" Multiple cries of my sister's name sounded from downstairs, and I suddenly became aware of the loud chatter and bustle below.

"And that's our cue to leave," Rahima grinned. "Do you want me to keep this in my drawer for now or do you want to put it in your room before we leave?"

I returned my gaze to the frame and decided then and there what to do. "I'm going to take it with me."

"What?"

"I want to take it to the wedding." I hastily shoved the frame back into its wrapping.

Rahima raised her eyebrows in confusion, but more calls frantically calling her name prevented her from saying anything else.

I headed over to the door and held it open for her, watching as she followed me into the hall. I knew she was walking out for the last time as a single woman, but I also knew she would return as a married one, and that was okay because all that mattered was what we had between us. And that would never change.

Chapter 26
Ameerah

I analyzed my reflection in the full-length mirror. I wore my dark purple dress and silver climber earrings. My hair was in its typical half-ponytail style, except this time, instead of being directly on the back of my head, it was a little higher. Mama had given me a purple ribbon to fasten my ponytail with. I held my new shoes in one hand.

"Okay!" I announced loudly to myself. "I'm ready to go." I pranced out of my room, kind of enjoying the feeling of the soft cloth around my legs. Voices were coming from Abdel-Hakeem's room. Mama and Baba were in there, making sure Abdel-Hakeem looked perfect for his big day.

"Ameerah!" Ali called suddenly.

I turned and saw him standing at the base of the staircase, looking really sharp in his royal blue dress shirt and crisp black pants. He wore a royal blue and white tie around his neck. His hair, as always, was neatly parted off to the left side, his bangs combed away from his eyes.

I grinned as I made my way down. "Ali, you look great!"

"You do, too," Ali replied with a smile. "I would give you a hug, but Mama might yell at me for messing up your outfit."

"She won't notice." I gestured upstairs. "It sounds like a fashion show up there."

"Yeah," Ali laughed. "I bet Abdel-Hakeem's really excited."

"Too excited for his own good," I added, placing my shoes down beside the front door.

We headed for the nearest couch to sit on while we waited for the others. I sank into the soft couch, my legs dangling off the edge.

"Yeah. I'm happy for him." Ali paused and glanced at me. "Are you?"

I leaned into the couch, twiddling with my fingers. "What do you mean? Of course I am."

"You didn't seem too excited about it when he announced it at dinner that day."

"Yeah, because I was hit from a bunch of places with so much news that I didn't like!" I said emphatically. "Homeschooling, Sherine, being off the team, your job. All of that was just making me feel like no one cared about me or my opinions anymore. I couldn't listen to all that and then go and be happy about my oldest brother's wedding!"

Ali looked away. "I know this summer started off wacky, with... um, everything that's been happening, and I haven't really been there for you. I mean, I was paying too much attention to my job and didn't spend time with you at all. I even missed out on our health routine. Then there was the wedding prep, and that was all everyone was talking about."

He reached over and squeezed my shoulder. Surprised, I glanced at his hand, then slowly raised my eyes to his. I could see a friendly glint in those dark brown pupils. Ali gave me a small smile and continued, "But no matter what, Ameerah, you'll always be my little sister, my princess. Even though it feels like you're being forgotten, I do still love you. I promise."

I couldn't stop a happy smile from spreading across my

face. *Aww.* Straightening up in my seat, I laid my hands in my lap and answered, "Yeah, at first everything was super overwhelming and annoying. But now, I think, after everything that's happened, it was all for the better." I held up one pointer finger. "I mean, for one thing, Sherine will be back soon, insha Allah. And even though I hardly expected it, Hanaan might actually become a new friend. A close friend."

Ali nodded slowly. "What about... homeschooling?" he asked carefully.

I shrugged. "Apparently, there's a lot about it that I didn't know. And Hanaan helped me to see that it isn't as bad as people make it out to be, and to be more open-minded. So I'm going to give it a shot."

"That's good to hear. Speaking of shots, how do you feel about being off your team?"

I frowned a little. "I'm gonna miss it."

"You can still invite your team over to play here."

I nodded. "Yeah. Yeah, I can."

Ali adjusted his position. "Listen, everything happened all too suddenly and we're still in some messes, but that's okay. I guarantee you that everything has a solution, and good can come out of something we might thing is bad. Just wait and see."

He was right. I hadn't liked the idea of hanging out with Hanaan, but now that I was getting to know her, I found out that she was actually a really good friend. And exactly how many people out there liked pairing orange sorbet with strawberry cheesecake, anyway? I nodded again and gave my brother a real, genuinely happy smile.

Ali grinned and held out a fist. I touched mine to his, and at that moment, Ahmed came down the stairs, tugging at his collar. He wore the exact same royal blue shirt and tie as Ali. "Ugh," he muttered, walking towards us. "This shirt is too tight on me. It's making me itchy!"

"Oooh," I said, easing myself off the couch. "For once, Ahmed, you look decent."

"Oh yeah?" He paused, tugging at his collar to look me up and down. "I have to admit, you look okay too, for the first time in, like, ten years."

I laughed. "So you admit I was cute as a baby."

"You're missing the point, Ameerah!" Ahmed said. "You weren't even alive ten years ago."

"Ahmed, I'm *eleven!* Turning *twelve* in August!" I placed my hands on my hips. "I think that tight collar squeezed out every single brain cell you have."

"Nah, I just don't stuff my brain with 101 facts about Ameerah," Ahmed retorted.

"You don't stuff your brain with anything," I returned. "At least I know you're turning fourteen in November!"

"Break it up, guys." Ali stood up, placing his hands on both our shoulders. "You can argue after Abdel-Hakeem gets married." As he said that, my eldest brother strolled downstairs. He wore a black suit with a royal blue flower in his lapel, a matching shirt, and a black tie. His hair was neatly combed, shining in the sunlight streaming from the house's skylights. Mama and Baba followed behind him, beaming.

"Do I look good, guys?" Abdel-Hakeem asked, striking a

couple of poses.

"Abdel-Hakeem," Mama said. "Careful you don't wrinkle your suit!"

Ahmed snickered. "You look good enough to play a geek in a school play."

"Ahmed!" Mama turned on him with a stern look on her face.

"Says the geek himself," Abdel-Hakeem replied with a witty grin.

"Boys!"

Everyone burst out laughing. Baba patted Mama's shoulder.

"I think we're all set for the big day, Raabiyah," he said. "Let's get going."

Baba was dressed just like Ali and Ahmed. My father was the spitting image of Abdel-Hakeem, the only differences being his gray hairs, bald spot, and mustache. His eyes behind his thin rimmed glasses wrinkled at the corners from smiling.

Mama was wearing a dress in the same color as mine, but it had long sleeves and reached her ankles. Her wrists were adorned with one silver bracelet each, and she wore a silver hijab to match. Usually, her rounded face was alight with a smile, but right now she looked so concerned that her forehead was wrinkling.

"Oh... just a second, Waleed," she said, and rushed over to me. "Let's see..." She began analyzing me as if I were a piece of jewelry she was considering buying. "Oh, Ameerah, you look so cute!" she finally cooed, tapping my nose. "And Ahmed..." She turned to Ahmed, who, upon hearing his name, had stopped pulling his collar and looked up with a hopeful smile at Mama.

"Mama," Abdel-Hakeem cut in, looking at his phone. "Uncle Faiz just texted me that he and the others are on their way to the masjid."

"Good!" Mama replied, patting Ahmed's hair and his clothes. She analyzed his collar with a furrowed eyebrow and tried to fix it. "I haven't seen him or the others in months!"

"Oh, no!" said Baba, digging in his pocket for the van keys. "We're supposed to be at the masjid before the rest of our family arrives!"

"Aaahh!" Mama shrieked, standing up straight and completely forgetting about Ahmed. "Everyone get in the car!"

Abdel-Hakeem grinned. "They live an hour away, but yeah, let's get going."

He headed for the front door with Mama and Baba in tow. Ahmed's hopeful smile diminished.

"Oh, great," he muttered, pulling his collar again. "The sooner I get these clothes off, the better."

I giggled. I felt bad for my brother, but I couldn't help it.

"Oh, you won't be taking them off for a good couple of hours," Ali said with a laugh, and he followed the troop downstairs.

"Ugh, don't remind me," Ahmed remarked.

The Summer When Everything Changed

Epilogue

The wedding hall was a dazzling blur of bright colors and array of fabrics. A cheerful mood reflected off each of the smiling faces that surrounded the beautifully decorated stage in the center of the room, where the glowing bride and beaming groom sat across from each other. The imam sat between them, his voice magnified by the microphone attached to his shirt as he turned to Rahima, asking her if she would accept Abdel-Hakeem as her husband. Rahima's lips formed a smile as she said, "Yes." The imam repeated his question, and Rahima answered the same way. By the third time, Rahima had lifted her head triumphantly and declared, "Yes" in a loud, ringing tone. The imam then turned to Abdel-Hakeem with the same question.

Once the imam declared Abdel-Hakeem and Rahima to be husband and wife, a rousing cry of Allahu Akbar[18] resonated throughout the room. Family members and friends rushed to give congratulatory hugs to the newly wed, surrounding them in a tight circle.

A few hundred feet away, seated at one of the round decorated tables, were two young girls who had not spoken a word during the marriage ceremony. As they quietly watched the events unfold in front of them, the taller of the two gently nudged the other and slowly rose from her chair. Slightly confused, the other girl raised her eyebrows and followed as she walked out of the room.

Once they exited the hall and were standing outside in the shadow of the building, both girls let out breaths they didn't know they were holding and grinned at each other.

---

[18]God is Great

Ameerah broke the silence. "I guess we're related now, huh?"

"I guess so."

Ameerah hesitated before asking, "Was the crowd overwhelming you? Is that why you wanted to come outside?"

"Umm, a little, I guess. But I came outside because I wanted to show you something."

That's when Ameerah realized Hanaan was holding a package. A lumpy one, at that, but nevertheless, a package. It was covered in lovely golden wrapping paper, fastened in various areas with clear tape.

Ameerah raised her eyebrows. "What's that?"

"Look at what my sister gave me." Hanaan grinned and passed the package over to Ameerah. Confused, Ameerah took the package into her hands and analyzed it. After a moment of turning it over, she finally found the opening where Hanaan had previously opened it and gingerly slid her hand inside. She gasped as she slowly brought out the frame. "Oh..." she murmured, gazing at the dazzling new frame.

Hanaan nodded eagerly.

"I'm so glad you fixed everything with your sister." Ameerah raised her eyes to Hanaan's and beamed brightly.

"I am, too." Hanaan paused. "Rahima said you and I make a great team. You know, because we kinda worked together in this wedding business."

Ameerah slid the frame into its packaging and carefully handed it back to Hanaan. "When we were trying to figure out what was going on separately, we didn't really solve anything. But the information you shared with me and the information I shared with you actually helped the both of us. It helped everybody." She rubbed her right cheek. "Your sister's right."

"Yup, she is."

Ameerah held her hand up for a high-five. "We should keep

working together."

"I was hoping you'd say that," said Hanaan, completing the high-five.

Ameerah gave a side glance to the wedding hall. "We should go back in."

The two girls walked back inside the hall. It was dark, but the stage and tables were softly lit, the stage with blue and white lights, the tables with tall candles. Ameerah passed by the table where her brother Ali sat in his handsome blue shirt, and the siblings shared a smile. She and Hanaan quickly found a table and sat down. Everyone was huddled around Rahima and Abdel-Hakeem, offering hugs and taking pictures. Hanaan gazed at them, her face in her hands and a soft smile on her face. Finally, through a gap in the crowd surrounding the stage, Rahima's blooming face came into sight, and she caught Hanaan's gaze. Immediately, her face broke into a bright smile, and Hanaan willingly mirrored the gesture.

The fire from the candles flickered, playing with the shadows on the girls' faces. Ameerah and Hanaan shared a glance then. They smiled genuinely at each other. Hanaan raised an arm to wrap it around the smaller girl's shoulders. And as the rest of the wedding progressed, the two candles on the table continued to light up the faces of Hanaan Imraan and Ameerah Salleh.

Acknowledgments

Writing this book has been a great adventure for the two of us. Although separated by a physical distance of over 1,000 miles, our shared passion for our project has brought us together. We have loved bringing our characters and their stories to life, spending hours turning Hanaan and Ameerah into full-fledged, lifelike characters.

We have exchanged countless back-and-forth messages to come up with the story we wanted to tell. We certainly couldn't have done it without the wonders of the Internet, especially Google Hangouts.

We would like to acknowledge everyone who has helped us out at various points throughout our journey, offering advice, suggestions, and support.

Thank you to our editor, Safa, for her enthusiasm and encouragement.

Thank you to our friends who have encouraged us along the way.

Thank you to both of our families for their support: our parents, our siblings, and everyone else who has been bugging us to finish our book!

A special thank you to Nayma Kose and Juli Herman, our mothers who read multiple drafts of our manuscript and offered endless and honest feedback. You have supported us every step of the way and inspire us to put in our best work. We love you!

About the Authors

Nur and Nura are two writers who both aspire to revolutionize Islamic fiction and create powerful, relatable stories for Muslim youth (and coincidentally share the same name). Brought together by their shared love of creative writing, Nur and Nura have eagerly worked together to develop the exciting world of Ameerah and Hanaan.

Nura Fahzy is the second-born of four siblings. After 5 moves in 5 different states, she is currently settled in Texas. An American-born Malaysian, Nura studied digital art and design at North Lake College, Class of 2019. Her favorite color is pink, and her preferred ice cream flavors are coffee and chocolate. She enjoys drawing and making food.

Nur Kose is an American-Bengali-Turkish Muslim who is the eldest of five siblings. Nur has roots in upstate New York, Delaware, and North Carolina, where she studied English and Arabic at UNC-Chapel Hill, Class of 2019. Some of her favorite things are reading, snow, and ice cream (but not strawberry cheesecake with orange sorbet). Her favorite ice cream flavors are Snickers and banana split. She is also the author of the STAIRS series.

Follow Nur and Nura on their social media pages for more sneak peeks and updates on future content!

Facebook: The Two Lights
Instagram: thetwolights

Lost in my confusion, I walked back into the house. I was going to do more research, if that was all it took. I didn't like the idea of this wedding. I was tired of it. But Abdel-Hakeem was still my older brother, and despite the changes his decisions were making to my life, I couldn't let anything—or anyone—ruin his special day.

I hurried upstairs. I needed to use a computer, but I wasn't allowed to use Ahmed's (and who would want to anyway, considering the fact that he never cleaned it), and I couldn't raise any suspicions in Ali. Besides, he was napping right now. My last resort was Abdel-Hakeem's computer. His room was next to mine, yet separated by the staircase and held back by the railing. I turned left from the staircase and knocked on the shiny wooden door.

"Yeah?" Abdel-Hakeem asked.

"Ameerah," I said.

I heard the creaking of weight being distributed on a mattress, and then the door opened. Abdel-Hakeem stood in front of me, his hair a rumpled mess and his white shirt wrinkled where he had just been lying down. "Yo, Ameerah," he said. "What's up?" I mentally rehearsed my prepared dialogue. This was the first time in a long time I had actually "requested" to talk to him. Clearing my throat, I said, "If it's alright, I'd like to use your computer."

My brother raised a thick eyebrow. "Oh? How come?"

"Mama told me to start looking up homeschooling curriculums." I recited another line of dialogue from my artificial script. It wasn't a lie because she had actually told me that last week, and I had put it off since then. Until now, I guess.

Abdel-Hakeem shrugged. "Alright, then, by all means, go

153

ahead," he said, opening the door wider. He stepped aside to let me in.

I strode inside, worry creeping over me as I remembered that Abdel-Hakeem's desk and computer both faced his bed. Anything on the screen, Abdel-Hakeem would see if he just looked my way. And with him sitting on his bed, phone in hands, there was no way he couldn't secretly spy on me.

This was not planned. But I'll figure it out. Reluctantly, I sat down at the computer. I couldn't back out now. A feeling of self-consciousness crept over me as I opened a web browser. I typed in "homeschooling curriculums" just for cover, if Abdel-Hakeem did happen to look over my shoulder unexpectedly. I hastened to find a reliable page, and after a furtive glance over my shoulder at my brother, I opened a new tab and typed "Kathy Kramer wedding planner." As I scrolled down the page, I saw a lot of Facebook and Twitter pages, but none related to a wedding company of any sort. My brow furrowed, I went back to the search engine and erased "wedding planner." Now, with just Kathy's name in the search engine, I found a lot more reliable results. Facebook pages, Twitter account, student directory...

Aha! There it was. The tiny icon that represented the college Abdel-Hakeem had attended and graduated from. I clicked on it and scrolled down the page, skimming through the writing, until I got to a page which showed photos of graduated students, then current students.

My mouth dropped open, and I struggled to keep back a gasp to avoid raising suspicion in my brother, who sat unknowingly behind me. Quickly, I closed all my tabs, cleared my history, and closed the browser. "Uh, thanks, Abdel-Hakeem," I said hastily, struggling to get my legs out of the swivel chair.

"Found one?" my brother asked without looking my way.

"One what?" I asked, completely frazzled.

"Homeschool curriculum? I think that's what you were looking for."

"Oh. Right. Yeah." I gave him a quick wave of the hand. "Nah, results weren't really helpful. I, uh, probably gotta ask Mama for help." I shot for the door. "Gotta rush! Who knows homeschool curriculums better than Mama, y'know, huh?" Before my brother could respond, I closed his door and made a run for my room, my heart thumping wildly against my chest. I could NOT believe what I had just seen.

"Okay," I breathed heavily, walking in circles around my room. "Kathy Kramer is no one but a fraud. She doesn't work at that company called Her Ladyship's something or the other; she used to, but was *fired* from it! Lemme say that again. *Fired!*" I stopped pacing and seized my scalp. "Aahhh! I gotta tell somebody! But who do I tell? Abdel-Hakeem? Mama? Ali?"

I headed for my bed and flopped down on it. The only person I could tell was Hanaan! But how could I tell her? And what would she do about it? What would we do about it?

I grabbed one of my pillows and hugged it to my chest. For the first time in my life, I didn't know what to do.

Chapter 21
Hanaan

Ever since the day that Ameerah had come over with her mom and The Guy, I found myself in immense conflict about the whole idea that something was wrong with Kathy and the wedding planning. Ameerah's face kept forcing itself into my mind, her words ringing in my ears. I couldn't stop thinking about our conversation. If anything, her revelations had only served to confirm my suspicions, but was that a good thing or a bad thing?

I had been so upset that Rahima was getting married that I had never considered what I felt about the wedding itself. It was true that I didn't want the wedding to happen, but since it was already a fixed event, was I okay with the event itself turning out disastrous?

Finally, one calm afternoon when my parents were busy downstairs and Rahima was occupied with something in her room, I logged onto my mom's laptop, searching up Tres Belle Hotel in my browser. I entered the date June 21st in the booking section, and sure enough, Ameerah had been right. Big bold letters saying, "Booked for German Festival" popped up right at the top of the calendar.

So Ameerah was right, I thought, creating a new tab and searching "Botanica Flowers hours." I held my breath for the half second it took for the search results to appear on the screen.

Botanica Flowers is open every day of the week, except for Friday. Make your reservations now!

I breathed out slowly. I had already known this, but seeing